## DRO

Longarm unleashed two quick bullets at the thief's flying legs, and when the man collapsed in a rolling heap, Longarm raced forward, Colt at the ready. As he did so, the thief proved that he wasn't much smarter than his partner.

A derringer appeared in his fist, and even though the light was very poor, Longarm caught the glint of gun metal and instinctively fired.

The derringer barked like an angry bulldog. Longarm pressed his hand to his side and brought it away covered with blood . . .

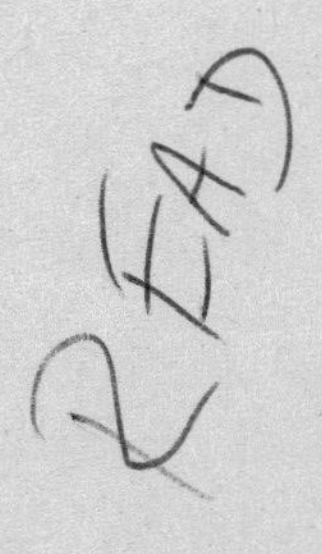

TABOR EVANS

J
JOVE BOOKS, NEW YORK

LONGARM AND THE BOUNTY HUNTERS

A Jove Book / published by arrangement with
the author

PRINTING HISTORY
Jove edition / July 1994



ISBN: 0-515-11407-3

A JOVE BOOK®
Jove Books are published by The Berkley Publishing Group,
200 Madison Avenue, New York, New York 10016.
JOVE and the "J" design are trademarks belonging
to Jove Publications, Inc.

PRINTED IN THE UNITED STATES OF AMERICA

10 9 8 7 6 5 4 3 2 1

# Chapter 1

"Thanks for meeting me on such short notice," Billy Vail said to Deputy Marshal Custis Long as they stood overlooking Denver's Cherry Creek. "This is important enough that I didn't want to talk to you at our office."

Longarm frowned. He was a tall, handsome man with a John L. Sullivan mustache and the deeply tanned face of a man who had spent too many hours out in the sun and wind. "What's wrong with the office?"

"Even our walls have ears."

Longarm raised his eyebrows in question, but said nothing. He knew full well that Billy was all business when it came to enforcing the law. Vail had been a deputy United States marshal just like Longarm and had been promoted out of the field, something he claimed had ruined him as an officer. "Custis, what I wanted to tell you is confidential."

"All right, shoot."

Billy had a bag of peanuts and he'd been feeding Denver's flourishing pigeon population. The pigeons were still swarming around them both. Longarm was wearing his good go-to-the-office suit and black Stetson. He kept glancing nervously skyward as Billy threw the damned peanuts into the air, trying to make one of the birds catch it on the fly.

"Come on, Billy," Longarm said, "we're gonna get shit on if you don't . . . Jezus! I told you it'd happen!"

Billy watched as Longarm dug a handkerchief out of his back pocket and tried to scrape the pigeon shit off his sleeve. The older man put the bag of peanuts away.

"Sorry about that," Billy said, struggling to keep a straight face.

"Sure you are!" Longarm snapped. "Now what the hell is so secret that we have to stand out here in the middle of a flock of damned pigeons?"

"Come on," Billy suggested, "let's go for a little walk. I've been putting on weight sitting at a damn desk day after day. I need the exercise."

"I don't *like* to walk," Longarm groused. "And I don't *need* any exercise."

"Walk anyway," Billy said, smile dying. "What I have to say isn't going to sit well with you."

Longarm had been about to complain some more about his soiled sleeve, but Billy's suddenly grave expression told him that there were much more important things in the wind.

"What's wrong?" Longarm asked. "Did some sonofabitch that I arrested and sent to prison break out and swear to come here and punch my ticket?"

"Not that bad," Billy said, head down and short legs striding out. "But bad enough."

"I'm in no mood for guessing games," Longarm said, pitching his handkerchief into a trash can and thinking how much he disliked sea gulls and pigeons. They were easily the most worthless damned birds in existence.

"I've some troubling news about Marshals Berry, Denton . . . and Heck Wilcox."

Longarm stopped and his hand shot out to grab his boss by the forearm. Heck Wilcox was like a father to Longarm. "What about Heck? Has he been shot up again?"

"No," Billy said, removing Longarm's hand from his sleeve. "Heck is just fine. Fact is, he's prospering."

Longarm found that difficult to believe. Heck Wilcox was known for always being broke. He was an old lobo wolf and wilder than a wolverine, but he was a good lawman and generous to a fault. Everyone expected Heck to die of lead poisoning without a cent in his pocket.

"You say Heck is prospering?"

"That's right." Billy glanced sideways at Longarm. "I know how much the old man means to you, Custis. And I know that he saved your life when you first became a marshal."

"And taught me about being a lawman," Longarm added. "But how the deuce can you say that man is 'prospering'? Not on *our* pay, he ain't."

"Well, that's the point," Billy said. "He sent in his resignation along with Marshals Berry and Denton."

Longarm stopped. "What?"

"That's right. All three of them resigned about two months ago."

"Well, why didn't you tell me?" Longarm shook his head. "Berry and Denton were sort of misfits anyway. I never knew why Heck even bothered to give them the time of day out in Nevada. But . . ."

"They turned in their badges to become bounty hunters," Billy stated bluntly, not even attempting to hide his contempt. "That's why they're starting to prosper."

Longarm stopped and turned to face his boss. "Billy, are you sure?"

"I'm afraid so. I've got their letters of resignation in my office, if you want to look at them. They sent them along with a note and a little surprise package."

"Surprise package?"

"Yeah," Billy said. "They cut off and sent us the ear of One-Eared George."

"Are you serious?"

"I wouldn't joke about something like that," Billy said. "I'll show you the ear if—"

"That's all right," Longarm said quickly. "I just don't understand why Heck would do such a thing."

"His note and the federal wanted poster pretty much explains matters. It says that One-Eared George was worth three hundred dollars dead or alive, and that the reward is to be paid out of this Denver office. Heck says he trusts that the ear will leave no doubt that he got his man and that he, Berry, and Denton have decided to go into business for themselves."

Billy sighed. "Along with the ear and the note of explanation, they also sent in their badges."

"I sure am sorry to hear this," Longarm said. "Heck always took his oath of office seriously, and said that being a deputy United States marshal was a proud calling."

"I know. I worked with Heck right after the war. It was in Texas, and I looked up to him almost as much as you."

"How old do you think Heck is?"

"Pushin' sixty-five."

"I sure don't understand this," Longarm said. "And I'd like to see Heck's note."

"It's his handwriting," Billy said. "I already checked. There's no doubt about that."

"Dammit, Billy! I just can't believe that old Heck Wilcox would actually quit the service. How long was he a federal marshal?"

"Twenty-three years. Long enough to get a dollar a month pension for every year of service."

"Twenty-three dollars a month isn't even beer money for a man with Heck's thirst."

"I think that's why him and them other two jumped into the bounty business."

Longarm drew a nickel cheroot from of his coat pocket. He bit off the tip and jammed it into his mouth. Many times he just chewed them to a nub, but right now he lit and inhaled the cheroot, his thoughts dark and disappointed.

"I expected better of Heck," Longarm said quietly. "I knew that he was nearing the end of his string as far as being a marshal. Billy?"

"Yeah?"

"Heck wasn't ever going to get a promotion, was he?"

"No," Billy confessed. "Heck never would listen to me or anyone else. He was rough and had a tendency to take the law into his own hands. Rules meant nothing to him, but I always knew he could be counted upon to do the tough jobs, just like you, Custis."

Longarm knew he'd just received a high compliment, but it didn't raise his spirits. He felt lousy because being a bounty hunter was about the lowest thing a former officer of the law could become. A bounty hunter was a pure mercenary. Unless the reward on the head of the man or men he hunted specifically stated that they were to be brought in alive, a bounty hunter could shoot them in cold blood and claim his reward without the responsibilities of watching over or feeding his prisoners. Bounty hunters were a breed apart; most were really commissioned assassins.

"I sure can't believe that old Heck would stoop that low," Longarm said quietly. "How the hell come you didn't tell me sooner?"

"I was hoping that Heck would change his mind and you'd never have to know. I thought maybe he was just drinking and acting crazy and that he'd come to his senses."

"But he didn't."

"No," Billy said. "In fact, he and the other two have turned out to be a real embarrassment to the department. More than an embarrassment actually."

Longarm looked up sharply. "What does that mean?"

"One-Eared George had made a deal with the governor of Nevada. He was to have received a full pardon."

"He was?"

"That's right. And furthermore, I have a telegram saying that George was caught along with two of his gang members and all of them were beaten to death."

"I don't believe it!"

"I can show you the telegram." Billy rustled around in his coat pockets, which were always rat's nests. "Hang on," he said, "I got that telegram right here someplace."

Longarm waited while Billy unfolded the telegram and handed it to him. The message was from no less than the Nevada governor to the governor of Colorado and the tone was, to put it mildly, acid.

> DEAR GOVERNOR STOP THREE FORMER DEPUTY UNITED STATES MARSHALS OPERATING OUT OF FEDERAL COURTHOUSE IN DENVER HAVE DECIDED TO TAKE PROFIT FROM THE LAW STOP FORMER DEPUTY MARSHALS WILCOX BERRY AND DENTON HAVE SET UP PARTNERSHIP WITH THE STATED INTENTION OF RIDDING NEVADA OF ALL WANTED OUTLAWS WITH BOUNTIES OVER FIFTY DOLLARS ON THEIR HEADS STOP WHILE WE APPLAUD THE CAPTURE OF MISCREANTS HORSE THIEVES MURDERERS AND THE LIKE I CANNOT CONDONE BRUTAL MANNER IN WHICH ONE-EARED GEORGE AND HIS TWO COMPANIONS WERE BEATEN TO DEATH STOP SINCE THESE MEN WERE FORMERLY UNDER YOUR STATE AS WELL AS THE

FEDERAL JURISDICTION PLEASE REIN IN THESE SELF APPOINTED VIGILANTES STOP

"He doesn't believe in mincing words, does he?" Billy said when it was clear that Longarm had read and then re-read the telegram.

"No," Longarm said, "he does not."

"I want you to go to Nevada and put a stop to this business," Billy said. "It's giving us a black eye and the governor is not one bit pleased."

Longarm had never refused an order, but he was on the verge of doing it now. "You know how I feel about Heck," he said awkwardly. "I think it would be far better if you sent another man."

"Why? You're the best that I have. Heck Wilcox may be old, but he'd eat any of my younger and less experienced deputies for breakfast. No," Billy said, "this is a job for the very best man I have available and that's you, Custis."

"Trouble is, Billy, I'm not sure that I . . . "

Longarm could not finish.

"Not sure you could what?" Billy pressed. "Arrest Heck?"

"Or worse. I'm damn sure that he'd never stand for being arrested. That wouldn't leave me a whole lot of room for peaceable options."

Billy frowned. "I see what you mean. On the other hand, if Heck has gone a little crazy, perhaps seeing an old and trusted friend—a man like you who was once like his own son—would jolt him back to his senses."

When Longarm still didn't look convinced, Billy played his last hole card. "Look at it this way. Either you try and talk him into his senses, or Heck is going to run afoul of the law and either get shot or get his neck stretched."

Longarm thought about that for about ten seconds before he nodded his head in agreement. "All right. You make a good point, and I'll take the first train to Nevada."

"Good!" Billy reached into his inside coat pocket. "As a matter of fact, I've already taken the liberty of buying a ticket."

"First class?"

"Second class, which is a lot better than third class."

"Yeah, in second class the board seats are painted so you don't get splinters in your ass when you try to stretch out on them and catch a few winks."

Billy chuckled. "It isn't that bad, Longarm."

"Yeah, well, it ain't that good. How soon does my train leave?"

"In about three hours."

"Thanks," Longarm said drily. "I don't suppose you've requisitioned me any traveling money."

"As a matter of fact, I have. Two hundred dollars, in addition to the price of your train ticket."

Longarm's eyebrows raised in question. Even for going clear to Nevada, that kind of money was extremely generous, and neither Billy Vail nor the United States Government was known for its generosity.

"How come so much?"

"I think that this job is going to be hard and dangerous. And frankly, I don't think that you're going to have much luck converting any of our three fallen deputies back to the straight and narrow."

"What about the reward money for One-Eared George?"

"You're taking that to them—with our stern warning as well as that of the governor of Nevada."

"That sure isn't going to make talking them back into government work any easier."

"Who said we'd take them back?"

Longarm blinked. Billy was dead serious. "I'll do what I can," Longarm said.

"Good. Heck is worth saving, if he hasn't poisoned his mind yet with bad whiskey, mescal, or whatever. The other two—just watch out for Berry and Denton. I wouldn't turn my back on either one of them."

"I've ridden with both men," Longarm argued. "I've been in some hard scrapes with them and they're capable."

"Capable of killing you," Billy said darkly. He turned and resumed walking toward the Federal Building.

Longarm fell in beside him, and Billy added, "I think Berry and Denton have become like wild dogs."

"What's that mean?"

"It means that once they've tasted blood—or real big money—they'll contract an instant craving for more. Savvy?"

Longarm savvied plenty, and his ruminations became as dark and troubled as those of his boss as they headed back toward the Federal Building to take a look at the bloody ear of One-Eared George.

# Chapter 2

Longarm prepared to board the Denver Pacific for the run up to Cheyenne, where he would catch the Union Pacific Railroad, which he could ride all the way to Reno. In Reno, he would rent or buy a horse, saddle, and outfit, then travel on down to Carson City to pay his respects to the governor. Marshal Billy Vail had made it very clear that the governor of Colorado, as well as his own boss, expected some Nevada peacock feathers to be smoothed. Longarm was not a man who enjoyed being a peacemaker, but that too was often part of his job.

"Custis!"

Longarm turned to see Billy hurrying to catch him before he boarded the train, which was about ready to depart.

"Custis," Billy wheezed, red-faced and badly winded. "Here's the federal reward money for One-Eared George. I guess, if nothing else, this ought to attract our three ex-marshals to your side."

Longarm took the cash and counted it. "Three hundred is a lot of money," he said when he had finished and was satisfied that the count was accurate. "But split three ways, maybe it's not so much of a reward."

"Couple of months pay," Billy said, trying hard to catch his breath. "You should point out to those three the danger of their new ways and the rewards and personal satisfaction of government employment."

"Funny," Longarm said drily, "but right at the moment, I can't seem to think of a single damn government reward or personal satisfaction."

Billy didn't appreciate his deputy marshal's dry humor, but seemed to decide that there was no time for a lecture. "Oh, one other thing, Custis," he said, digging into his pocket. "This is Heck Wilcox's badge. Maybe seeing it again will help you talk him into coming back into the fold."

"Maybe." Longarm took Heck's badge. It had been worn so long and hard that the silver was starting to wear thin. Longarm stared at it and ran his thumb over its worn finish. "What about the other two badges?"

"I think I'll keep them," Billy said after a long pause. "At least until this matter of the fatal beatings is cleared up to our satisfaction."

"Yeah," Longarm said, "that might be a good idea."

Billy stuck out his hand. "You take care of yourself and watch your backside. I'll be here, and the telegraph line can get any messages back and forth between us faster'n either one of us can think to write 'em."

"Yep."

The train's big steam whistle screeched a warning to the passengers who had not yet boarded. Longarm shouldered his saddlebags and bedroll. "So long, Billy."

"Custis, I wish I was coming along with you. I tried, but the big boys won't unchain me from my damn desk."

Longarm could see that his boss really did want to come along and help. To cheer him up, Longarm scoffed and said, "Aw, hell, Billy. You'd just get in my way or slow me down. Maybe get yourself plugged."

"I can still ride you into the ground!"

"Sure you can," Longarm said, with a wink of his eye as he climbed onto the train and waved goodbye. He stood on the platform between the third- and second-class coaches until Billy disappeared from sight. Secretly, he wished that Billy was coming along too. Confronting Heck Wilcox was going to be one of the hardest things that Longarm had ever had to do, worse by far than having teeth pulled by some damned dentist.

With Denver receding into the distance, Longarm made his way down the aisle of the second-class coach, but then the train suddenly lurched forward. Longarm was just in the process of slipping around a prosperous-looking but rotund man when the train's sudden motion threw him off balance. Grabbing wildly for the overhead luggage compartment rail, Longarm toppled over onto one of the already seated passengers.

"Oomph!" the passenger gasped. "You big oaf, would you please get off my lap!"

He twisted around, his face inches from that of a very attractive young woman with red hair and green, angry eyes. "Yes, ma'am!"

Longarm hesitated only a moment, and then he reached over to grab the back of the next seat and pushed himself to his feet. The woman looked furious, and was busily straightening her lavender and lace dress.

She glared at Longarm with stern disapproval and said, "Sir, have you been imbibing?"

"Beg your pardon?" he asked, removing his Stetson.

"Drinking! Have you been drinking?"

"No, ma'am! I only drink beer and whiskey unless the saloon is out of both. In that case, I drink—"

"Never mind!" The young woman said, waving her hand as if she were shooing pesky flies. "I don't care what you do or do not drink. Just . . . just don't bother me again."

Before Longarm could apologize for a second time, the woman raised a newspaper up to hide her pretty face. That, Longarm thought, was a real pity. "Sorry, ma'am. Be happy to make it up to you somehow."

"Then leave," she said in a cold voice.

The heavyset man raised his eyebrows and glared at Longarm with an air of disdain. He was probably in his early thirties, with chipmunk cheeks, double chins, and a gold watch and chain that would have bought a small house in Denver.

Clearing his throat and shaking his sagging jowls, the man said, "I think that the young lady would like you to move on, sir. You are probably lost."

"Lost?"

"Yes, I'm sure that your train ticket is for the third-class coach. That's the next car back."

The arrogant man stood, removed his expensive bowler, and actually bowed before saying, "Miss, please excuse this man's ungainly behavior."

"Shut up!" Longarm snapped. "I can make my own apologies. But the fact is, if you weren't so chubby, I'd never have had to wedge myself around you and then I wouldn't have gotten jerked off my feet by the train."

"Well, sir!" the passenger said imperiously. "I think I need to speak to the conductor of this coach about your appalling lack of good manners."

"You can speak to whoever the hell you want," Longarm said. "But mister, I don't care how much money you have because you'd better understand that I'm a United States marshal."

"You're a lawman?"

"That's right."

"Then why aren't you wearing a badge!"

"Because I have enemies and I enjoy ownin' the element of surprise when I meet the lawless."

"Well," the man grumped, "from what I hear, there are an entire nest of miscreants residing in the third-class coach. They drink, they use the profanity in the presence of . . . females, and they are a despicable lot. Why don't you go back there and make them behave themselves?"

"They've paid their train fare," Longarm said, feeling his patience slipping, "and unless there is some kind of trouble, I'll leave them to their own devices."

The fat man's nose wrinkled, pig-like. "What is your name and who is your superior?"

"It's Custis Long and my superior is Marshal William Vail in the Denver federal office."

The man pulled out a silver pen and a notebook. He glared at Longarm and said. "Vail. Is that spelled

V-A-L-E or V-E-I-L or V-A-I-L?"

"Figure it out for yourself," Longarm said. "What are you doin' in second class, slumming?"

The heavyset man recoiled. "Good day, Marshal," he spat, twisting around and making a big show of waddling forward to the first-class coach.

Longarm looked down at the green-eyed woman. "I can't stand snobs, can you, ma'am?"

"It's *miss*," she said curtly. "And I don't like strangers—period. Now, if you will leave me to my reading and find your own seat?"

"Sure." Longarm tromped on up the aisle, and finally found an empty seat up near the front of the coach. Passengers in second-class enjoyed the small but important comfort of upholstered seats instead of the hard wooden benches that the poor third-class passengers were forced to suffer.

"Marshal Long!" the conductor said in greeting a few minutes later as he arrived to collect his ticket. "How far are you traveling?"

Longarm smiled to recognize Ike Meecham, a man in his sixties with a shock of silver hair and a sunny disposition. Ike was unflappable and very competent. Longarm and the conductor had spent many an enjoyable hour discussing life, famous outlaws, and gunfights. The older man had a real interest in the passing of the Wild West, and always spoke sadly about how there were no longer any herds of buffalo to be seen from the coaches.

"Goin' all the way to Reno, Ike."

"Good! But wasn't it just last month that you traveled with us?"

"Yep. Had a little trouble over in Laramie. That's a rough town."

"It is," Ike agreed. "A railroad town, and I mean no disrespect to my fellow trainmen, but they can be rambunctious and quarrelsome on paydays."

"I know," Longarm said. "Who was that big, self-important fella with the twenty-pound solid-gold watch and chain?"

"That was Mr. Edwin Nettles. His father is one of the principal stockholders in this railroad and young Edwin is his only heir. If you ask me, they're a pretty blue-blood crowd, Marshal."

"I can't speak for the father, but I sure didn't like the son," Longarm groused. "I don't know how you put up with a fella like that."

"I don't," Ike said. "I let the conductor who serves the ladies and gentlemen up in the first-class coach do it. He probably earns twenty or thirty dollars worth of tips, but by the end of the run, he's so upset by the way he's been treated that he drinks up that extra money."

Ike chuckled. "I don't go after that extra money but I also don't suffer from ulcers, indigestion, and heartburn."

"I think you're smart."

"Glad someone does. My wife says that I keep working just so I don't have to listen to her gossip in the daytime and snore at night."

Longarm laughed. "Is that true?"

"I'm afraid it is," Ike admitted.

"Who is that pretty red-haired woman whose soft lap I landed in a few minutes ago?"

"You landed on Miss Chambers?"

"I did. Who is she?"

Ike leaned closer so that he could not be overheard even though the pounding of the rails underneath them was enough to drown out all but a loud conversation. "Miss Chambers is the daughter of Colonel Ezra Chambers, one of Nevada's most celebrated newspapermen and journalists."

"For a fact?"

"Yes. I hear he has bought a newspaper in Carson City." Ike chuckled. "And I also heard that the colonel wasn't in the state capital one day before he got into a shouting match with some crusty old senator from Elko County. The two old birds flew into a rage and went at each other with their walking canes!"

Longarm chuckled. "Really?"

"Yep. And Miss Chambers seems to have inherited her father's miserable disposition, wouldn't you agree?"

"I'm afraid that I would," Longarm said, "but she's still mighty pretty."

Ike snorted. "Down South I once saw a coral snake. Beautiful thing with bright colors. I said to myself that it was the prettiest snake I ever did see—but in the same breath, I told myself to steer a wide berth because, pretty or not—it was still poisonous."

"I hear what you're saying," Longarm agreed, settling back in his seat. "But when it comes to young red-haired and green-eyed women, I am like a moth drawn to the flame."

The remark was intended to make Ike laugh, and it exceeded beyond Longarm's expectations.

Ike patted his shoulder and said, "We're going to have a good trip, Marshal. A good trip."

"Do you want to know why I'm going to Reno?" Longarm asked.

"You can tell me?"

Longarm nodded. In a few terse words, he told Ike about Heck Wilcox, Berry, and Denton.

"I'm sorry to hear that about old Heck," Ike said, looking genuinely distressed. "Next to you, Heck was my favorite. That old man could tell the best stories I ever did hear. Tell them all night long, if he had whiskey to drink."

"I know."

"I sure hope that he realizes the mistake he's made and returns to his good senses and the fold," Ike said. "There are few things more despicable than a bounty hunter that kills for money."

"I agree."

Ike sighed. "But then, I reckon if Heck Wilcox had ten dollars for every man he's shot and killed, he'd be rich."

Longarm nodded because that was probably also true. Heck Wilcox might be old, but he was still a deadly, deadly man.

# Chapter 3

Most of the second-class passengers who traveled this line up to Cheyenne on a regular basis had brought little sacks of food. Within an hour of departure, the smell of fried chicken wafted enticingly through the coach, along with a number of other savory aromas. As usual, Longarm had forgotten to bring any food, and so he was forced to listen to his own stomach as it complained about him being so neglectful. Longarm tried to lean back in his seat and get a few hours of sleep, but it wouldn't come. He knew full well that their train would arrive in Cheyenne late that night, and then the passengers would be forced to hold over until they could be transferred to the Union Pacific line the following morning.

Longarm guessed that he could hold out for a meal until they arrived in Cheyenne, where several good cafes stayed open late in the hope of attracting hungry arrivals from Denver. He gazed out the window at the setting sun and thought of Heck Wilcox. That old man had had a powerful influence on Custis. In fact, it had been Wilcox who'd convinced him that he ought to be a federal lawman. That was right after Wilcox had survived a savage gun battle down in a little Texas town named Amarillo. Heck had seemed old even then, and his hair had been gray, but his hand had been a streak and his aim true as he'd dropped three cutthroats who'd refused to be apprehended by a single run-down-looking hellion of a federal marshal.

Longarm's thoughts were interrupted as the door to the coach opened and Mr. Edwin Nettles filled the aisle. He looked down his nose at Longarm and then passed up the aisle.

Longarm twisted around to see Nettles standing next to Miss Chambers. He couldn't hear the conversation, but it was brief and ended with the young lady shaking her head in a firm refusal, probably declining a sumptuous dinner in the first-class coach. Longarm beamed. Good for her!

He turned around, expecting the heavy man to pass back through the coach. When he did not, Longarm twisted around again to see that Edwin was still pestering Miss Chambers.

"Enough," Longarm muttered to himself. He removed his marshal's badge from his coat pocket and pinned it on his lapel, then smoothed his hair and climbed out of his seat into the aisle.

"Is this man bothering you, Miss Chambers? Because if he is, I'll take care of him right now."

She did look beleaguered by Edwin Nettles's persistence, but said, "No, thank you, Marshal. I believe Mr. Nettles was just leaving."

Nettles was not one bit happy. "Well, if you chose to go hungry, then that is certainly your choice, Miss Chambers. But—"

Longarm grabbed the heavy man by the seat of his britches and the collar of his coat. It was all Longarm could do to spin the wealthy fool around and propel him back up the aisle to the applause of the other second-class coach passengers.

"Always at your service, Miss Chambers," he said, starting to turn around and return to his seat.

"Marshal, please wait a moment."

Longarm turned and gave the lady his best smile. She *was* lovely. "Is there something else that I can do for you, Miss Chambers?"

"No," she said. "I just wanted to apologize for my angry and ill-advised words after you fell on me. I'm not usually so rude. I had no business being so nasty. I'm afraid that I behaved very badly, and I've no excuse except that I am under a good deal of pressure."

"I see." Longarm gestured to the empty window seat beside her. "May I join you for a few minutes? Perhaps there is something that I can do to ease your worries."

She scooted over next to the window. "I'm afraid that would be impossible, Marshal . . ."

"Long. Custis Long. A servant of the people, and especially of lovely and troubled young women."

She blushed and extended her hand to Longarm. "I'm Katherine Chambers, and I really do prefer to be called Katherine, not Kathy."

"I'll remember that, Katherine," Longarm said, taking a seat beside the lovely creature. "And what is it that would trouble one so beautiful as yourself?"

"Really, Marshal, I have no wish to burden a stranger with my life's trials."

"Burden me."

Katherine looked closely at him. "It's my father," she said after a moment. "I have a letter from him in Carson City, where he purchased a newspaper. He's such an irascible old man, but a sweetheart under all his thunder and bluster. I'm his only child."

Katherine's eyes misted. "You see, my mother died of cholera about ten years ago and my father went to pieces. I was sent to live with my Aunt Edna in Philadelphia, and then to a very fine girls' finishing school."

"It shows."

"Not in light of my poor earlier manners."

"Forget that," Longarm said earnestly. "A big stranger fell on you and you were startled, perhaps even hurt. Katherine, *were* you hurt?"

"No," she quickly assured him. "Just startled and upset by my father's last letter. He almost got killed! He challenged a Nevada senator to a duel. Can you imagine?"

"Yes," Longarm said truthfully. "Passions run very high out there."

"I don't know what I'm going to do when I see him," Katherine confessed. "He's too old and crotchety to be starting another newspaper. I had thought he would choose a comfortable and well-deserved retirement. Maybe write a few editorials for some other newspaper. He had money, but now he's spent it all on this Carson City paper. If it fails, and from what I read between the lines it very well might, then my father will be penniless."

"I see."

Longarm noticed that the girl had no concern about any possible inheritance or her own future, only about her father. It increased his already considerable admiration for Miss Chambers. "Are you going to Carson City to try and help your father run his newspaper?"

"Or sell it if any buyer can possibly be found."

"But what if he refuses to sell? It may well be that he can't be happy without owning his own newspaper. If that's the case, what will you do then?"

She threw up her hands in exasperation. "I've never been able to reason with him or change his mind. He is the most obstinate, stubborn man that I've ever known."

Longarm suspected that Katherine shared some of those same characteristics, but was wise enough to keep this opinion to himself. "If your father refuses to sell out, what will you do?"

"I honestly don't know," she admitted. "I have many friends in Denver, and there is someone rather special."

Longarm had been afraid to hear something like this. "A fiancé?"

"No, my grandmother."

"Well, that is something to think about," Longarm said with an inward sigh of relief.

"Yes, but she is a little addled," Katherine said. "In fact, she rarely even remembers who I am anymore. The dear woman is almost one hundred years old. Fortunately, my father left her well provided for. That's like him to take care of his mother even as he slips into financial ruin."

Longarm could see that Katherine was genuinely upset about her father's situation. "Perhaps his newspaper will prosper and everything will turn out fine."

"I hope so. I'm going to do everything in my power to help see that it does."

Longarm nodded, pleased that his optimistic words seemed to have lifted her spirits. When she asked him about his past, Longarm told her that he was originally from West Virginia and, before becoming a federal marshal, had worked as a cowboy, "rust eater" on railroad construction crews laying track, and hardrock miner.

"Did you mine on the Comstock?"

"As a matter of fact, that was one of the places that I worked."

"I understand that the Comstock Lode is in decline," Katherine said. "My father writes to say that production of gold and silver has fallen."

"That's true, but there are new gold and silver strikes taking place all over Nevada. Cities like Carson City and Reno are, of course, going to weather the ups and downs of the mines. The boom towns keep sprouting up like mushrooms in the spring."

"I've never been to Nevada. In fact, Marshal, I've never been west of Denver."

"Custis," he corrected, laying his hand comfortingly on her arm. "We're going to be traveling together for quite some time and might as well drop the formalities."

She smiled. "I'm so glad that you came to join me. Mr. Nettles was very insistent that I join him for supper up in the first-class dining car. And to be honest, I was tempted. They're having roast pheasant, antelope steaks, corn on the cob, fresh fruit, hot rolls—"

"Please," Longarm begged, "I'm about half starved myself and I'd rather not hear about all the wonderful delights that those people are about to enjoy."

"You didn't bring any food either?"

"No. But as soon as we arrive in Cheyenne, how about I buy you a big steak dinner with potatoes, rolls, and apple pie for dessert?"

"It sounds wonderful. But I really couldn't."

"Why?"

"Well, I know that a federal marshal isn't exactly overpaid. I wouldn't dream of accepting your generous offer."

"I've plenty of travel money. Join me, please."

She smiled and looked deep into his eyes. Longarm felt his heart skip a beat, and then his pulse quickened when she said, "Very well, Custis."

"Good!"

Longarm didn't remember the rest of their train ride up to Cheyenne, except that he forgot he was hungry and the time flew by, making the journey seem as if it took but minutes. He discovered, among other things, that Katherine was an aspiring journalist and wanted to someday write novels of the Wild West. However, instead of just writing about hunting and shooting and Indian fights, she intended to introduce a little romance.

"I mean, cowboys, miners, freighters, and all those rugged people *do* fall in love with something besides their mules and their horses, don't they?"

"Why, sure!"

"See?"

Longarm debated whether or not he should tell Katherine that women were mighty scarce in the West, especially young, pretty, and *respectable* women. The kind of woman that were most often found in the frontier towns were not the kind of women who sought romance. Instead they used their soiled charms for the accumulation of hard cash.

"Perhaps I could write a story about *you*, Marshal Long."

He blushed. "I doubt that would be very interesting, and I'm afraid that my job discourages romance."

"How so?"

"Well, take this trip, for example. I'm also on my way to Carson City, where I may have to arrest three former federal officers who have become bounty hunters."

"Really?"

"Yes, and one of them was like a father to me. He still is. I don't know what I'll do if I should have to face him in a showdown."

"My goodness! That could actually happen?"

Longarm thought of Heck Wilcox. "Yes, it could. This man is every bit as stubborn as your own father, Katherine. Try and tell him to do one thing and you can almost bet that he'll do the opposite."

"Then tell him you approve of him trading his badge in for the status of a bounty hunter."

"I can't," Longarm said. "He'd know that I was lying. Either that, or he'd ask me to join him and the other two I have to confront."

Katherine shook her head. "It sounds like you are heading for even more trouble and possible heartache than I am. And here I've been bemoaning my own small troubles when you face three men!"

"That's all right," Longarm said, taking Katherine's hand and looking deep into those green eyes. "If I'm killed, well, at least I have had a chance for a little romance—thanks to you."

It was Katherine's turn to blush, but she did not pull her hand away. Instead, she held Longarm's hand as their train thundered north toward Cheyenne.

"Is it true that we have to wait until tomorrow morning before we can board a westbound train?" she asked as Ike came through to announce that they would be arriving in Cheyenne in fifteen minutes.

"I'm afraid so."

"I suppose that I can remain at the train depot. That must be what most of the passengers who are transferring to the Union Pacific elect to do."

"The westbound doesn't leave until ten o'clock in the morning," Longarm said. "That would make a very long night and morning. I know an excellent hotel close by."

"Would they have two rooms?"

"I'm sure they would."

"Not too expensive, I hope. You see, I'm embarrassed to say that I am a little short on funds. Otherwise, I would have ticketed on the first-class coach."

"But then we wouldn't have met and you'd be suffering the company of Edwin Nettles."

Katherine laughed. "Why, that's exactly so!"

Longarm patted Katherine's hand. "I'm really glad that we had a chance to meet. It's going to make the trip far more pleasant, and I want you to enjoy yourself and not worry about a thing. I'm going to see that you have a very good time."

"Thank you," she whispered, squeezing his hand. "I confess that I was concerned about this trip. I saw the third-class passengers loading and they are a pretty rough lot. I saw women with babies forced to endure that group."

"Most third-class passengers are emigrants or people temporarily down on their luck. Some are fortune-seekers traveling to the very Nevada boom towns I told you about. There are a few bad apples in that barrel, but by and large they are fine, hardworking folks simply hoping for a chance to better themselves."

Katherine smiled. "Marshal, you really are a kind-hearted and quite eloquent man when you speak about something that you care deeply about."

Longarm swelled with pride and anticipation. He might have one hell of a bad time when he found Heck Wilcox and the other two former marshals, but he was going to enjoy this long train trip thoroughly.

# Chapter 4

Longarm had a real interest in the history of the West, and he knew a little about the founding of Cheyenne, which he was pleased to share with Katherine.

"The town was named after the Cheyenne Indians by the Union Pacific's chief engineer, General Grenville Dodge. I read an interesting story that said he camped there right after the Civil War and decided that it would make an excellent terminus for the Union Pacific."

"I've heard that it has an enormous roundhouse for the repair of locomotives," Katherine said. "And that most of the people who live in Cheyenne are employed, in one fashion or another, by the Union Pacific."

"Not quite true. There are some very large cattle ranches in this country, but without the financial impact of the Union Pacific, Cheyenne would be just another jerkwater town."

"Jerkwater? What a strange term. Where did it come from?"

"In small and isolated rail towns, there is always a water tank and the engineer is forced to jerk a rope to fill his own boilers."

Katherine laughed. "I see!"

"Cheyenne has always had a colorful reputation, but also a romantic one. You can still see cowboys and Indians on the streets, and visit the stockyards to watch cattle by the thousands being loaded into boxcars and sent to the Eastern markets."

"And are there still shootouts on the main street?"

"Sometimes," Longarm said. "Saturday nights can be pretty wild. You wouldn't want to be walking around on the streets all by yourself, Katherine. There are quite a few pickpockets and thieves that make their living preying off unsuspecting railroad passengers who have to wait over for either an eastbound or westbound train."

"I've got my own private United States marshal to protect me."

"That's right," he said agreeably. "If we had some time, I'd show you the capitol building of the territory."

"I'm afraid that's not going to be possible, unless we both agreed to meet early tomorrow morning for a stroll about the town."

"Now there's an idea," Longarm said without enthusiasm.

The train came to a halt at the station, and Ike Meecham greeted them both. "They got the stove burnin' in the station, if that's where you want to wait until we board for Reno."

"I think that we'll try and get hotel rooms," Longarm said. "Miss Chambers is tired, and you know we've got a long trip ahead of us."

Ike waited until he alone had Longarm's eye, then winked and said, "Excellent decision. I'd do the very same, if I were you, Marshal."

"Thanks," Longarm said with a half smile as he escorted Katherine off the train and onto the busy passenger dock and loading platform.

"I have a small blue trunk that contains a few things I need for tonight," Katherine called out loudly to the departing conductor.

"Don't worry, ma'am!" Ike said, turning on his heels and coming back to them. "If our good friend Marshal Long will follow me, I'll give your trunk to him right now. That way, there is no chance of a mix-up. The rest of your baggage will be transferred onto the westbound so you don't have to worry about a thing."

"You are very nice," Katherine said, opening her purse and pressing change into the conductor's palm.

"Well, thank you, Miss Chambers," Ike said before turning to hurry down the platform.

"Wait here and I'll be right back," Longarm said.

"It's not a big trunk, really it isn't," Katherine assured him.

"No problem."

Longarm threaded his way through the crowd as he hurried after the conductor. They stopped at the baggage coach, and both waited impatiently for several minutes as the baggage from Denver was loaded onto a wheeled baggage cart.

"That's it," Ike said, pointing to a blue trunk that was about the size of a Wells Fargo strongbox.

Ike grabbed the trunk and started to pull it off

the cart, but then stopped. "Marshal Long, why don't you just take it?" he suggested. "I'll just go along and look after the rest of Miss Chambers's luggage."

"Heavy, huh?"

"A little."

The trunk must have been filled with lead or a block of granite. As Katherine had promised, it wasn't large, but it had to have weighed at least a hundred pounds. Longarm grunted and scooped it up into his arms. He was strong, but there were so many people clambering about on the platform that it was not an easy task to wend his way back to Katherine.

Longarm bumped into someone.

"Oops, excuse . . . oh, it's you, Nettles," Longarm groused, realizing that he'd bumped into the rotund man. No doubt Mr. Nettles had already hired someone on the dock to carry his expensive leather luggage off to Cheyenne's finest hotel for the night.

The rich young man said, "We had a splendid supper we enjoyed this evening. Too bad you and Miss Chambers went hungry."

Longarm pushed up against the heavyset man, and then he dropped the heavy trunk on Edwin's toes. One moment the wealthy and obnoxious man had a sneer on his round face; the next moment his mouth formed a big open circle and he screamed.

"Ooowww! My toes! You . . . you broke them!"

"I'm so sorry," Longarm said with a faint smile as he stooped to pick up the trunk.

Edwin couldn't seem to stop hollering. Everyone on the loading platform turned to watch as the roundish fellow danced up and down, causing the floor to shake. Everyone, that is, except Longarm, who hurried away to find Katherine.

"Help!" she cried. "Custis! Help!"

Longarm dropped the ponderous trunk and ran to the woman's side. There were tears in her eyes and, like Edwin Nettles, she was jumping up and down, but for a very different reason.

"Two men grabbed my purse and ran that way!" she cried.

"Those two?" Longarm shouted, pointing to a pair of men who were jumping off the dock and running toward town.

"Yes!"

Longarm took off after the pair. He was in good condition and his long legs had always served him well as a swift runner. The two crooks didn't even realize that they were being followed, and Longarm gave them no warning until he rapidly overtook them.

"Halt!" he shouted when he drew near. "Federal marshal! You men are under arrest!"

The pair whirled, saw Longarm, and went for their side arms. Longarm skidded to a halt and went for his well-oiled six-gun. He carried his double-action Colt on his left hip butt forward, and his draw was extremely quick. His gun came up and he fired in one smooth blur of motion.

The first man went down hard, but the second was smarter and faster. He scooped up Katherine's purse, ducked behind a wagon before Longarm could get a clear bead on him, then sprinted for an alley.

"Halt or I'll shoot!" Longarm bellowed, going after the thief.

The man didn't halt, and Longarm had no choice but to fire or the thief would have escaped with

Katherine's purse. He unleashed two quick bullets at the thief's flying legs, and when the man collapsed in a rolling heap, Longarm raced forward, Colt ready and waiting.

"Hands out in front of you!" Longarm ordered.

But the man was gripping his bloody pants leg. "I need a doctor!"

"You'll have one," Longarm said, bending to grab Katherine's purse in his left hand.

As he did so, the thief proved that he wasn't much smarter than his partner. A derringer appeared in his fist, and even though the light was very poor, Longarm caught the glint of gun metal and instinctively fired at the exact same instant that the derringer barked like an angry bulldog.

Longarm felt the derringer's slug crease his ribs even as he pulled his trigger once more and the man at his feet was hammered backward against the dirt.

"Dammit," Longarm muttered, pressing his hand to his side wound and bringing it away covered with blood.

He wasn't badly wounded, but Longarm knew that the derringer's slug had furrowed his rib bones and would give him a lot of grief on the train trip west. It was just the kind of gunshot that kept a man in a constant state of discomfort.

Longarm stared down at the dead man. He didn't recognize him as being wanted for any federal offense. Not surprising since stealing purses was hardly a major crime. A quick search of the dead man revealed that he carried no identification, again not surprising.

"Get the sheriff," Longarm ordered when a few

men hurried over to gawk at the dead thieves.

"Sheriff got hisself gunned down last week," one of the men admitted a little sheepishly.

"All right, then get the undertaker," Longarm said, cradling Katherine's purse under his arm and heading back to the depot to calm her fears.

# Chapter 5

"You've been shot!" Katherine cried in alarm. "Oh, my God, you're bleeding!"

"It's all right," he assured her. "It's just a flesh wound. All I need is some bandaging up. I've cut myself worse trying to shave. Here," Longarm added, handing Katherine her purse.

Katherine's hand flew into the purse and rummaged around for a moment. "It's gone!"

"What's gone?"

"I had money! Three hundred dollars!"

Longarm heaved a sigh of disappointment. "I'll bet they reached inside and that's the first thing they found before they even got off this passenger dock. I'll go back and see if one of them still has your money on his body."

"I'll go with you," she said, grim-faced. "But I'm not very hopeful."

In truth, neither was Longarm. He strongly suspected that the bodies had been looted almost as soon as he left them behind. This suspicion was sadly confirmed a few minutes later after Katherine had followed him to each of the still-warm bodies, keeping her eyes averted from the dead men.

"Katherine, I'm very sorry," Longarm said when he'd rifled both men's pockets and come up empty. "I had no idea that your money would be that quick or easy to find."

"I was foolish not to have kept my money hidden on my person," she said, looking dejected. "It's my fault. You did everything possible."

"At least you've a train ticket," he said. "And I've plenty enough traveling money to get us where we're bound."

"I can't take your government money!"

"Sure you can. It's all right, Katherine. I promise you, we'll do just fine."

"Let's find a doctor," she said. "I'm so sorry that you were wounded."

"I'll be all right," he assured her. "It's just a flesh wound and I've some bandages in my saddlebags."

"You carry bandages?"

"Just in case," Longarm said quickly. "I carry a lot of things in my saddlebags. You'll find handcuffs, a telescope, and much, much more."

"I see."

Longarm spotted one of the young men who gathered each time the train arrived to try and make some tips moving people and baggage. The man was leaving the depot empty-handed. Longarm signaled him.

"We left a blue trunk up on the loading dock. I want it delivered right now to the Four Queens Hotel, where we'll be staying overnight."

"But I can't pay for a room!" Katherine protested.

"I'll pay for it. Come along. We've had enough excitement for one evening."

While the young man hurried back to the train depot in order to retrieve the trunk, Longarm took Katherine up the street to their hotel. He was a frequent guest and knew the hotel clerk on a first-name basis.

"Good evening, Fergus."

Fergus was a slight, ascetic young man with a quick smile and a woman's delicate hands. "Good evening . . . Marshal, you've been shot!"

"Just creased. Fergus, this is my friend and companion, Miss Chambers. We're waiting for tomorrow's westbound train, and we need a couple of rooms for the night."

"And a doctor, I'm sure."

"No, I'll be fine."

Fergus didn't look convinced, but knew better than to argue. "Marshal Long, we can have your coat and shirt cleaned and pressed and ready for you by tomorrow morning? I'm sure that you'll want those bloodstains removed before you board the Union Pacific."

Longarm examined his coat. It had been unbuttoned during the shooting and he was glad to see that the bullet had not ruined it. The shirt was another matter entirely.

"Very well, let's have the coat cleaned—cold water for the blood, Fergus—never hot."

"Yes, sir. Both shirt and coat?"

"The shirt is a lost cause."

"I agree, sir." Fergus accepted Longarm's coat, and drew in a sharp breath when he saw the blood matted at Longarm's side.

"Good heavens," Katherine whispered, growing pale. "Let's get you to a room and get that wound bandaged right now!"

"A room for me," Longarm said to Fergus. "And there will be a young fella coming with a blue trunk for Miss Chambers. Have him bring it right up."

"I'll have a bath and some hot water brought up at once. Anything else?"

"Whiskey," Longarm said, not caring if Katherine did disapprove of his request. "One glass."

"Make that *two* glasses and a bottle," Katherine corrected.

When Longarm looked strangely at her, she explained, "It isn't every day that a person gets robbed of all the money they have in the world and then sees the two dead men that did it. And Custis, this awful wound of yours, well, I just need a few jolts of whiskey to steady my frazzled nerves."

"Of course," Longarm said.

Fergus gave him a key, and Longarm allowed himself to be led up the hall to Room 14. Katherine's hands were shaking as she opened the door. "Remove your shirt and let's have a look at that wound."

Longarm did as ordered.

"Oh, my!" Katherine breathed. "It looks awful!"

"It's not," Longarm said. To assure her he would survive, he pointed out several bullet-wound scars.

"You're like a cat with nine lives," she said as Fergus hurried in with a porter, who brought whiskey and buckets of hot water to fill the huge tin bath.

Longarm tipped the desk clerk, and after the man from the depot arrived with Katherine's blue trunk, he closed the door. "Let's have a drink," he said, motioning toward the bottle.

Katherine poured them each a liberal glassful of whiskey. "To better days for the both of us, Custis."

"To better days," he echoed.

She finished cleaning the wound, and for the next hour they drank whiskey and talked, their mood and humor gradually improving. The whiskey hit hard, probably because they were both without food in their stomachs.

"I better get this thing wrapped," Longarm said, swaying to his feet, "but first, I'm not going to let that bath water go stone cold."

"You're going to take a bath?"

"Sure. That's an oversized two-person tub. Do you want to join me?"

Longarm said it half-jokingly, but Katherine took him seriously. "And if I do, what happens?"

"We get clean."

"And that's all?"

He laughed outright. "I don't know. That kind of depends on you, Katherine."

"Hmmm," she said, admiring his muscular body. "I guess it might at that. All right. What the hell! I've never bathed with a man before, much less a wounded United States marshal. I'd guess that would make quite an exciting chapter in my first frontier romantic novel, wouldn't it?"

"We'll see," Longarm said, refilling their glasses and kicking off his boots.

When he unbuckled his gunbelt and stepped out of his pants, Katherine's eyes became very large. "My, my!"

"What does that mean?"

"It means that you *are* long in more than name."

He chuckled and climbed into the tub. "Come on, Katherine, the water is getting cold."

Katherine was a little on the shy side. She turned her back to him while he sipped on the whiskey.

"You're going to have to face me when you get into this tub," he said.

"I know." Katherine's underclothes dropped to her feet. She stepped free of them and slowly turned around.

"Wow!" Longarm grinned broadly. "Would you look at those beauties! Katherine, you are sure one hell of a good-looking woman!"

"I am?"

"You know you are," he said, setting his glass down and extending his hand.

Katherine climbed over the rim of the tub. She shivered and squatted down in the tepid water. "It really isn't very hot anymore, is it?"

"No, but I've got a solution."

"You do?"

"Yes. Come over here."

She raised her eyebrows in question. "You mean, on top of you?"

"That's right. There isn't room for you to slip in alongside, and my poor ribs wouldn't take that anyway."

Katherine reached for her own glass of whiskey. Her eyes were bright, and her hands no longer trembled. "I can't believe I'm really in this tub with a frontier lawman."

He reached for her, and Katherine's legs parted as she knelt over him. He looked into her green eyes, and then he gazed hungrily at her large and pendulous breasts. "They're beautiful."

In reply, she leaned forward so that they dangled before his face. Longarm took one in his hands and squeezed it gently, then took her nipple into his mouth and began to stimulate it with his tongue.

Katherine moaned with pleasure. She wrapped her arms around him and pressed closer. Longarm reached down and guided his rapidly stiffening manhood into her. Katherine moaned even louder and sat down hard, hips starting to rotate as he slipped deep inside her and began to stir her passions with his wet, pulsing shaft.

"Talk about frontier romance," she whispered, nipping at his shoulder. "We're just getting acquainted and already we're making love."

"And isn't that nice," he said, driving even deeper into Katherine until her bottom began to surge up and down.

"Yes," she breathed, working on his rod with increasing intensity.

The bathtub began to overflow. Longarm reached for his whiskey and took a long drink, then set his glass far enough from the lip of the tub so that no bath water sloshed into his drink. By now, Katherine was really starting to get excited. Her breathing was coming very fast, her body pistoning wildly up and down on his big shaft.

"Oh, Custis," she groaned, "I don't think we need a second room."

He gripped each of her butt cheeks in his strong hands and began to twist her a little until she squealed with delight. "I'd guess not, Katherine."

By the time that they both exploded into a thrusting frenzy, they'd sloshed most of the bath water across the floor. Katherine was crazy with desire, and Longarm was as well. His wound had started bleeding a little again, but he didn't care. All he cared about for the moment was making love to Katherine Chambers and giving her something worth remembering and writing about.

In the morning, they made love twice more, and Wyoming's territorial capitol building be damned. They could see it when they grew old and had nothing better to do. Katherine was a tiger in bed, really quite insatiable, and if not for his aching side and the troubles that awaited both of them in Nevada, Longarm would have suggested they miss the westbound train and stay in their room for about another week until they were spent from lovemaking.

"But we can't," Longarm said. "We've got responsibilities in Nevada."

"Will you stay with me in Carson City?"

"No," he said, "I can't. What would your father think?"

"He's a man. I think he'd accept you."

"Maybe, but maybe not. And besides," Longarm argued, "this trip is a chance for you and your father to work out some serious problems. You can do that much better with just the two of you."

"I suppose," Katherine admitted, "but I can't bear to think that this is the last time that we'll make love."

"It isn't," Longarm said. "I'm going to figure out ways for us to sneak off and find a great many passionate moments to share before we even reach Nevada."

"How?"

"I have friends in high places on this railroad."

"Not Mr. Edwin Nettles, I'd judge," Katherine said with an impish grin.

"No, not Nettles. In fact, I rather doubt that he'll be proceeding any farther."

"But why?"

When Longarm told her about how he'd dropped the blue trunk on the man's toes and probably broken them, Katherine howled with laughter. "It serves the clod right!"

"Yes," Longarm agreed, "it does."

They managed to make love once more before leaving the Four Queens. This time they did it fully dressed and on a last-minute impulse. Longarm lifted Katherine's dress and pushed her underclothing down to her ankles, then backed her up against their door and gave her one final lusty poke.

"My goodness!" she said, trying to smooth her thick red hair and gather her wits after he'd finished and was buttoning up his pants. "Marshal, you're a glutton!"

"For you, I am," he admitted. "You have the same effect on me as chocolate candy. One taste and I've got to have a whole lot more."

Katherine smiled. "Good," she said, rearranging herself and then smoothing her dress. "I was wondering about something."

"Yes?"

"Do you think it would be too dangerous to climb up on the roof of our passenger coach and make love?"

"While the train is moving?"

"Of course. Otherwise, what would be the point?"

"None, I guess. But I'm afraid that it would definitely be too dangerous. That's one that you'll have to leave out of your frontier romance novel."

"Oh, well," she sighed, "I've a fertile mind. I'll think of other unusual places."

"I certainly hope so," he said, touching the fresh bandage at his side. "Just as long as they are not too athletic and I don't have to go into some kind of contortionist act."

"Oh, no," she assured him, "I promise that I won't forget about your ribs. It's that other part that I'm now constantly thinking about."

Longarm felt his cheeks warm. "With a little effort, you could be pretty brazen, Katherine."

"With you, it doesn't take any effort whatsoever."

Longarm guessed that was a pretty nice compliment. "Let's go," he said.

# Chapter 6

Longarm and Katherine did not see a sign of Edwin Nettles that morning after breakfast as the passengers boarded the Union Pacific train to travel westward.

"I understand he is still howling and has two of Cheyenne's doctors in his constant attendance," Ike Meecham, who was standing on the platform waiting for his own train to return to Denver, said with the bare hint of a grin.

"I pity the doctors," Longarm said.

"Don't," Ike advised, "They'll charge Mr. Nettles a small fortune for their services. However, you might be a little concerned about your own welfare."

"What does that mean?"

"It means that Mr. Nettles is threatening to have you arrested for assault and battery."

Longarm shrugged. "It was an accident. Miss Chambers's heavy trunk slipped out of my hands, and unfortunately, Mr. Nettle's toes were where the trunk happened to land."

"You might convince a judge, but not me," Ike said.

Suddenly the Union Pacific conductor cupped his hands to his mouth and shouted, "All aboard! Next stop is Laramie, Wyoming! Then Rock Springs and all points on to Sacramento! All aboard!"

Longarm started to escort Katherine to the train when a heavy hand fell on his arm. "Custis Long?"

He turned and looked at the tall, beefy man who had stopped him. He was dressed in a brown woolen suit and gray Stetson. About Longarm's age, he had the look of a lawman or private investigator.

"Yes?"

"Mr. Nettles has signed a warrant for your arrest for assault and battery."

"Let me see it."

The man reached into his coat pocket and unfolded the warrant. "As you will see, it has been issued by a county judge and is in order."

Longarm studied the warrant for a minute before he handed it back to the man. "I'm a federal officer and I'm on duty," he said. "I've business to take care of in Nevada."

"Too damn bad. I'm saying that your business will just have to wait."

"No," Longarm said, "it won't. Federal authority supersedes local authority. And while we are talking about authority, what is yours?"

"I'm . . . I'm a private agent."

"A 'private agent'?" Longarm glanced sideways at Katherine, then back at the tall man. "What exactly does that mean? That you've been hired off the street by Mr. Nettles to attempt to detain me?"

The man leaned closer. He was bull-necked and broad shouldered, with a fist-busted nose and the look of a brawler. "Why don't you make this easy for both of us and come along peaceably, Marshal? I'm just doing my job."

"Sorry," Longarm said, reaching for Katherine's arm, "but I'm also trying to do *my* job. That means that I have to catch this train."

"Ain't gonna happen," the big man said, brushing his suit coat aside and shading his gun.

The heel of Longarm's boot smashed down on the man's instep, and, at the same time he whipped his right elbow up and back. It caught the big man in the solar plexus and doubled him up gasping for air.

"Tell Mr. Nettles I'm going to Nevada."

"You sonofabitch!" the man cried, straightening and taking a swing at Longarm.

Longarm ducked the punch and stepped inside. His right fist slammed upward into the man's solar plexus a second time, and when his mouth flew open in agony, Longarm followed through with a wicked left uppercut to the point of the man's jaw. He went crashing over backward and began to writhe on the platform.

"Find a new occupation," Longarm said, "Serving warrants on federal marshals is not your strong point."

The man just groaned in answer and whooped, trying to suck air into his lungs.

"Did you hurt him quite badly?" Katherine asked when they were on board.

"No. Just his pride and probably his pocketbook. I imagine that he isn't going to get paid by Nettles when the man discovers that I am on a westbound train."

"No," Katherine said, peering out the window as they moved up the aisle to see if the beaten man was still rolling around in agony on the loading platform, "I would imagine not."

Longarm and Katherine found a seat in the second-class coach and made themselves comfortable. They were both so spent from the night of making love that they fell asleep almost the moment the train left Cheyenne on a long climb over the heavily forested Laramie Mountains.

As the days passed, Longarm and Katherine enjoyed a wonderful trip. The weather was cool but invigorating, and Longarm was able, for a small gratuity, to obtain the privacy of an unused sleeping berth for many blissful hours of lovemaking with Katherine.

When they passed through the Echo Tunnels and climbed over the Wasatch Mountains into Utah Territory, Katherine was thrilled to see the great Salt Lake Basin shimmering like snow in the far distance.

"It's beautiful!" she exclaimed. "I had no idea that this Mormon country was such a paradise."

"They've done a lot to make it so," Longarm said. "Brigham Young and his followers are the most industrious people I've ever known. I'm told that, when they first arrived, this country was little more than sagebrush. All along these western mountain slopes they've built farms and communities. The Mormons are well ordered and clean-living. They'll tolerate no saloons, no drunken gunfights, or even profanity. Theft is almost unheard of in their close-knit communities."

"It sounds like a cultural Utopia."

"A what?"

"Utopia means a place that enjoys a perfect political and social system where everyone lives happily ever after."

"Oh." Longarm frowned. "I sure wouldn't go that far. These people practice polygamy, and I can imagine that it doesn't sit well with every wife."

"No," Katherine said, gazing out at some distant city far to the south, "I'm sure that it doesn't. Tell me, Custis, have you ever married?"

"Nope."

"Do you ever expect to marry?"

"I dunno," he confessed. "A home and family isn't in the cards for me as long as I remain a federal marshal."

"Maybe you should consider other lines of work that would give you the chance to marry and raise a family."

"Maybe," he said without enthusiasm. "But I enjoy what I do and I'm damn good at being a federal lawman."

"But it's dangerous, the hours are impossible, and it doesn't pay very much. You've told me all of this several times in the last few days."

"I have?"

"Uh-huh."

"Well," Longarm said, "I didn't realize that I was talking like that about my line of work. I guess I am sort of down on the job right now because of what awaits me in Nevada."

"You mean with those three friends of yours who became bounty hunters?"

"Yes. But only one of them qualifies as a friend. The other pair are just acquaintances. Jim Denton and Billy Berry never were the kind of men that I'd enjoy riding into a fight with."

"Why not?"

"I dunno," Longarm said, "They were both just a little too quick to fly off the handle, to pull the trigger, to throw a punch. I've never backed off from a fight, Katherine, but I believe the best way to handle trouble is with talk. If talk fails, *then* you go to the next step."

Katherine touched his cheek. "You really are an unusual man, Custis. The thing that I find so appealing is that, despite the violence you have experienced, you've still a gentleness inside of you."

"I do?" It was the last thing he'd expected to hear her say after the whipping he'd delivered to the big man who tried to arrest him back in Cheyenne.

"Yes." She bent close to whisper in his ear. "But you're certainly not gentle in the bathtub, or the bed, or that sleeping berth."

Longarm smiled. Just thinking about riding Katherine to the sway of the train was enough to cause his pants to peak.

After the Great Salt Lake and its salt- and alkali-covered basin, Nevada was flat and covered with sage. The train stopped in Elko and several other towns before it finally arrived in Reno. Longarm suspected that he and Katherine were the only two passengers on the entire westbound train that were sorry to end their journey.

"Hope to see you both again," the conductor said as he pulled Katherine's luggage aside.

"All that's yours?" Longarm asked Katherine with astonishment as his eyes took in the huge mountain of boxes, trunks, and baggage.

"I'm afraid so," she said, shrugging her shoulders innocently. "It's everything that I own in this world."

"It's enough for six pretty young ladies."

"Perhaps, but it's not that far to Carson City, where I'll find my father and live in his new home, is it?"

"About thirty miles." Longarm scowled. "I'll rent a buckboard and we'll load it all up and haul it down to the capital."

"Thank you," she said, batting her eyelids and evaporating his annoyance like misty fog in summer sunshine.

Longarm rented a buckboard for six dollars, a ridiculously high price, but one that he had to accept because he was in a hurry to reach the state capital before darkness.

"You goin' to kill anyone in Carson City?" the liveryman asked in a hopeful tone of voice.

"Not likely," Longarm said. "Why you askin'?"

"No special reason. Just seems like you kill a couple of fellas every time you come to Nevada."

"Well," Longarm said, "I'll try my damnedest to change the pattern this trip."

"You gonna bring old Heck Wilcox and them other two ex-federal marshals up short?"

Longarm scowled. "I'd guess not. There's no law that says men like Heck can't quit the agency and go right to work for themselves."

"As bounty hunters?"

"Why not?"

The liveryman shook his head. "I dunno, but if you asked me, it just has a bad taste."

"Well," Longarm said curtly, "no one asked you."

The liveryman was taken aback by Longarm's curt reply. "I didn't mean no disrespect or insult."

"None taken. Where can I return this buckboard and team of horses?"

"Anderson's Livery. Mort Anderson owns it and he's my brother-in-law. Good enough fella."

"I know the place," Longarm said, hopping up into the wagon and driving it back to the train depot, where Katherine was waiting.

After Longarm loaded Katherine's huge pile of boxes, trunks, and baggage into the wagon, they drove down Virginia Street and over the Truckee River bridge, and then threaded their way through heavy street traffic until they left Reno heading south. It was a beautiful autumn day and the leaves of the many trees along the city streets were turning brilliant fall colors.

"This is magnificent!" Katherine said, sitting close beside Longarm and hugging his arm. "And look at those snow-capped mountains!"

"Yeah," Longarm said. "They've had an early snowfall up on the Sierras."

A few miles out of Reno they drove past a field of bubbling mineral hot springs that smelled like sulfur and sent ribbons of steam rising into the clear, cool sky. As they passed them, Katherine said, "Do you suppose that we could pull over and hike up into those springs and take a bath?"

"We'd burn our butts off," Longarm said. "Besides, I doubt we'd have much fun rolling around in the salt and minerals that cake the ground all around those springs."

"You're probably right."

When they entered Washoe Valley, Katherine was

completely won over by the beauty of the western Nevada country. Washoe Lake gleamed in the late afternoon sun like polished silver. Mountain shadows crept over the tall ponderosa pines along the west rim, and raced toward the barren, sage-covered hills to the east of the lake.

"This country has such a rugged majesty to it," Katherine said, feeling the chill of the afternoon as a breeze played with tendrils of her hair. "Custis, exactly where is the famed Comstock Lode?"

Longarm pointed to the east and a low set of barren-looking mountains across from the shallow but large Washoe Lake. "Just over those mountains. The Comstock Lode was discovered in 1859, and it's the richest gold and silver strike that's ever been found."

"Bigger than the gold strike in California ten years earlier?"

"Yep. A lot bigger. Big difference between the two. Over in California, they placer-mined."

"What does that mean?"

"It means that they panned the gold out of rivers and streams or picked it out of quartz deposits. But on the Comstock Lode, it was all deep, hardrock mining. Why, mines like the Ophir and the Bonanza went down a thousand feet or more."

"Really?"

"Yep. I worked in one where you went down in a damned steel cage suspended from a wire cable. When it dropped, it left your belly on top and sent your ass straight to hell. The temperatures were well over a hundred and got hotter the deeper you mined. It was a miserable job, but I was real young and the money was great—three dollars a day."

"Not enough," Katherine said. "Not for being dropped into a hellhole."

"There were a lot of damned good miners that died in those deep mines," Longarm admitted. "Sometimes when I go up to Virginia City, I still stop by their big cemetery and visit some of my old friends."

"Tell me about Carson City."

"I don't know a lot about it," Longarm confessed. "The town was named after Kit Carson and founded well after Reno was prospering. For a long time, everyone thought that Virginia City would become the state capital. It was a beehive of activity, and I'd guess there were more than thirty thousand people on the Comstock during its heyday."

"How many now?"

"Last I saw, about five thousand and falling with the ore production. But fifteen or twenty years ago, the people up on the Comstock thought that they were sitting on a mountain of gold that would never be mined out. They argued that Virginia City, being the territory's largest city, ought to be the capital."

"Then why didn't they prevail?"

"I think wiser men realized that strikes come and they go. Carson City is supported by agriculture and there are a number of big ranches and farms in the surrounding area. It's sort of a trading center for this part of the country, and I like the town very much. Despite the falling off of the Comstock, Carson City seems to keep on growing and prospering."

"Well, that's encouraging. I can hardly wait to see my father again. He's going to be very surprised."

"Didn't you tell him that you were coming?"

"No," Katherine confessed. "He would have asked

me to remain in Denver and take care of Grandma. But I just couldn't. I love my grandma, but my father comes first."

"I understand," Longarm said. "I just hope that this works out well for you and you're not setting yourself up for a very big disappointment."

"I'm not," she assured him. "I know my father better than anyone. He is cantankerous and outspoken, but he's also a man of integrity possessing excellent taste. I'm sure that he purchased a very nice home and needs some help cooking and cleaning. If I stay, however, I'll be looking for work."

"Maybe you can help your father run his newspaper."

"Maybe, but I doubt it. He's difficult enough being around when he's at loose ends. I can't quite imagine being around him all day long while he's working."

"Oh."

"And what about you? How will you find your old friend Heck Wilcox?"

"No problem there," Longarm said cryptically. "Wherever Heck chooses to be, people are generally scattering. He is his own best friend and worst enemy."

"I see. Then you expect Mr. Wilcox will be creating quite a stir?"

"I do."

Katherine sighed. "I just hope that you're not the one that is going to be hurt or disappointed. We can't ever change anyone, Custis. I've tried to change my father but failed. My mother spent her whole life trying to change him, but also failed. It sounds like

Heck Wilcox is the kind of man that won't change either."

"I'm not comin' to change him," Longarm said. "But I do expect him to obey the law and behave himself. And if he steps across the line into lawlessness, I'd rather it be me that comes down on him and turns things around than some stranger."

"I see."

"Do you?"

"Yes," Katherine said, "I do."

Longarm felt better then. "I'm sure lucky to have met you, Katherine. And I hope that this is just the beginning for us and not the end."

"So do I," she said, gazing ahead toward the hills that cradled Carson City.

When they topped a steep ridge that separated the green and verdant Washoe Valley from the sagebrush high desert of Carson City, Longarm pulled in the team to let the animals blow.

"There it is," he said, jumping down from the wagon for a moment to stretch his legs.

Katherine jumped down beside him. "My," she whispered, "it's so . . ."

"What?"

"Arid!"

Longarm chuckled. "I know that, after Denver and the greenery of Colorado, it does look pretty dry. But this country grows on a person. If you stay awhile, you'll come to love the smell of sage and the way the snow-capped mountains glisten in the moonlight. Being the territorial capital, there are lots of social and political things going on, and the best Fourth of July parade and picnic I ever attended. In the summer, you can take rides along the Carson River, and when the days get too warm, ride up to Lake Tahoe, the prettiest alpine lake in the entire country."

Longarm paused and blushed. "I didn't mean to make a stump speech or sound like the mayor."

"You didn't. Your words of praise for this area really lift my spirits."

"Good, because they ought to. Carson City is a real nice family town, Katherine. Your father knew what he was doing when he decided to live there."

"I just hope that he doesn't go broke or get himself shot in some silly duel."

"I'm sure that you'll have a moderating effect on him."

"What about us?"

Longarm toed the earth. "Katherine, you've your problems to take care of and I've got a bushel of my own to worry about."

"But we still can . . ."

"Yeah," he said, taking her into his arms and then kissing her mouth. "We still can and we still will, but maybe not every day."

"As often as you can come to me, I'll be waiting," she promised. "And if you need help, I'll be there for you no matter what."

"Same for me helpin' you," he said, feeling his throat tighten with emotion. "All you got to do is put out the word and I'll come runnin'."

Longarm held Katherine for several long and lovely minutes as the sun began to dive into the icy patches of snow along the highest peaks of the Sierras. Then he loaded her back into the buckboard and drove on down to find her father.

# Chapter 7

"Say," Longarm called out to a spindly-legged cowboy walking up Carson City's dimly lit main street that night, "Can you tell us where Mr. Ezra Chambers lives?"

"Last I heard, the old colonel either lives in the Washoe Saloon or in the back of his newspaper office."

"That's not true!" Katherine shouted from their wagon. "My father said he had a nice big Victorian house!"

"Fine, with me, lady," the cowboy said, "I'm just looking for a girl to dance and have a little fun with. You interested?"

"Mind your manners!" Longarm ordered.

The cowboy glared at Longarm and then dodged into a saloon. Longarm looked sideways at Katherine. "Don't worry, we'll find your father."

"There's the Washoe Saloon," she said, pointing to a place with a big sign just up ahead. "Maybe we should just stop the wagon for a minute and peek inside. Just in case."

"That's entirely up to you," Longarm said, feeling her growing anxiety.

"No, let's ask someone else."

"Fine." Longarm hailed a man who looked like a successful businessman and asked him the same question he'd asked the cowboy.

The man looked at them and proclaimed, "Mr. Chambers is either drunk or working on his rag at the *Carson Courier* office."

"And exactly where is the *Carson Courier* office?" Longarm asked, not one bit appreciating the man's choice of descriptive terms.

"Drive up to the next block and turn right. You'll see it two doors down. If Colonel Chambers is working, there will be a light on. But my guess is that he's drunk by now."

Longarm heard Katherine's sharp intake of breath and he wished he could reassure her, but from the comments he'd heard so far, her father had not exactly established himself as a pillar of propriety. And while Ike Meecham had called him a "celebrated newspaperman and journalist," Longarm was beginning to think that that was somewhat overblown.

"Oh, dear Lord," Katherine whispered when they were rolling again. "I can't believe that my father has fallen on such bad times!"

"Maybe he hasn't," Longarm said, trying to sound hopeful. "Maybe he just celebrates a lot."

Katherine glanced sideways at him and said nothing, so Longarm kept driving until they arrived at the front of the newspaper office.

"I see a lantern on inside," Katherine said. "But my father might have just left it on by mistake."

"Let's check and find out."

Longarm pulled the team of weary horses up and tied the lines around the brake, then jumped down and helped Katherine to the street. They walked up to the front door of the office and pounded on the door. The light died instantly.

"There's someone in there," Longarm said, pounding on the door even harder.

"Father!" Katherine yelled frantically. "Father, open up, it's Katherine!"

There was a long silence, and then Longarm heard something very heavy overturn and crash to the floor. Longarm was about to throw his shoulder to the door when a man inside bellowed, "I'm comin'!"

Longarm stood back, and it seemed to take forever before the door lock turned and a thoroughly drunk old sot appeared in the doorway.

"Katherine?" he asked, swaying back and forth while trying to focus.

"Father!" she cried, throwing her arms around the disreputable-looking old man.

They both would have toppled if Longarm had not grabbed and steadied them. "Easy."

"Father, what has happened to you?"

"What do you mean?" he asked, staggering back.

Longarm wanted to be somewhere else. The old man had probably once been a tall and rather commanding figure, but now he was just a shell of a human being. His cheeks were sunken, as were his eyes, which burned out of deep, dark orbs. He was thin and reeked of whiskey, and his clothes were soiled and rumpled. Colonel Ezra Chambers looked more like an everyday drunk than a distinguished newspaperman or journalist.

"Why'd you come out here?" he cried, clearly appalled to see his daughter. "Katherine, you shouldn't have come!"

She hugged him and sobbed until the old man began to cry too. Longarm decided it would be best if he returned their wagon. "I'll be back as soon as I see these horses get taken care of," he said quietly.

He found Anderson's Livery, and when he asked Mort about Colonel Chambers, the liveryman's lip curled. "That old man came here with all the show in the world. He was throwin' his money around like a politician just before the election. Bought a big Victorian over on the west side of town and a pretty nice little newspaper office."

"What happened to him?"

"He's in poor health," the liveryman said. "I heard that he has a cancer. He just went downhill pretty fast. I guess he's in a lot of pain and the laudanum prescribed by the doctor isn't strong enough to cut the pain. He drinks too much, and when his newspaper began to fail, he just sort of gave up."

"But we found him in the newspaper office. I took a quick look around and it appears to still be in operation."

"Oh, sure, the colonel still puts out a biweekly, but it ain't worth the paper it's printed on. Mostly it's just gossip, and he has a few of his last remaining friends writing silly pieces."

The liveryman worked at the hitches of the horses. "Colonel Chambers can't even find boys that will peddle his damned paper anymore. Nobody buys it except the colonel's friends lookin' for their own names, and there ain't many of them left."

"That's a sad, sad story."

"Sure it is," the liveryman agreed. "When he was feelin' good, the colonel was a hell of a man. He was crusty and outspoken, but people listened when he spoke. And the man could write as good as anyone whose words ever blessed a Nevada editorial. He was respected by the governor, the senators, and the state assemblymen. Everyone in the capital looked up to Colonel Ezra Chambers."

"But that all changed."

"Yes, the cancer is taking him down in a big hurry. There are plenty of folks that think that he ought to just shoot himself because it would be an act of mercy compared to drinking himself to death."

"Are you one of them?"

"No," Anderson said, "I am not. I believe the Good Lord gave us all life and he's the only one that can take it back."

"I see."

"How'd these horses behave themselves?" Mort said, inspecting the team.

"Fine. They work well together."

"What about all that luggage and them trunks and stuff in the back of the wagon?"

"Put them in the barn where they'll be safe, and I'll come back for them tomorrow when we figure out where Miss Chambers will be staying."

"Miss Chambers? You mean the colonel has a daughter that's come to Carson City?"

"That's right."

Mort Anderson shook his head. "I hope she's damn well heeled because her father is sure in a bad fix."

Longarm was feeling so discouraged by the news of Ezra's cancer that all he could do was wag his head in sympathetic agreement, even though he knew that Katherine was dead broke and had been depending on her father for a place to sleep and food to eat until she could get established.

"Marshal, what brings you to Carson City?" Mort asked.

"I'm looking for three fellas named Heck Wilcox, Jim Denton, and Bill Berry. Are they in town?"

"No, thank God!"

"That bad, huh?"

Anderson nodded. "Let's just put it this way. They've long since worn out their welcome."

"I see. Any idea where they are right now?"

"Probably raisin' hell up on the Comstock. I dunno. They got our sheriff totally buffaloed. When they ride into town, he rides out of town."

"He's scared of them?"

"Scared to death! Old Heck beat the livin' bejezus out of him one day. Happened right out on the street so that everyone could watch. Since then, Sheriff Wilbur hasn't been worth a damn. Even a rumor of Heck comin' round is enough to send him runnin' like a coon chased by hounds."

"He needs to resign."

"Yep, but no one is willin' to take his place. They're all afraid that old Heck will beat the shit outa them too."

Longarm understood what the man was saying because Heck Wilcox, gray hair or not, could be pretty intimidating when he wanted. Furthermore, he was a heller in a fistfight and was an expert with a gun or a knife. Only a fool would brace Heck Wilcox, drunk or sober.

Longarm left Anderson's Livery after helping to unload all of Katherine's luggage and storing it in a safe place inside the barn. What he'd heard about Colonel Chambers left him wondering what he could do to help Katherine. Maybe there wasn't a damn thing he could do. Maybe Katherine was just going to have to find some inner reserves and a way to make her father's last few days, weeks, or months bearable.

When he returned to the little newspaper office a short while later, Katherine had cleaned her father up and even gotten him to change his shirt. The old man still looked like death, but he seemed to have at least gathered his wits.

"I'm pleased to meet you, sir," Longarm said after Katherine had introduced them.

"No, you aren't," Chambers snapped. "You was probably hopin' for a man with money so you could marry my daughter. Now you've found out I'm just a broke, dyin' drunk."

"Father! Don't say such cruel things!"

"It's all right," Longarm said. "The man is feeling sorry for himself and he's given up the fight and resigned himself to death."

A spark flared in Chamber's dull eyes. "Why you big sonofabitch! If I was your age, I'd kick your ass from here to Reno and back for sayin' that."

"Why? It's the truth, isn't it?"

"Get out of here!" the old man shouted, raising a shaking fist. "Get out before I find my gun!"

"I think you'd better go," Katherine said.

"Why don't we *both* go," Longarm suggested. "I'll get us a room and—"

"No," she said firmly. "From now on, I'll be staying here at the office."

Longarm looked around the room. There was an ancient Washington printing press, with stacks of papers and clutter most everywhere else. He saw empty whiskey bottles lying in a litter of chicken bones, and judged the place was so filthy that even cockroaches would leave in disgust.

"Are you sure?" Longarm asked.

"Yes. Why don't you go about your business and come visit me after a few days?"

Longarm was a little taken aback. "All right," he said, "I will. Your trunks and luggage are over at Anderson's Livery stowed away in an empty stall. Mr. Anderson promises me that everything will be safe until you need it."

"Good."

Longarm walked outside and Katherine followed. He turned and reached for her, but she stepped out of his grasp. "If you took me in your arms, I'm afraid that I wouldn't have the courage to stay with my father. So please don't."

"All right." Longarm shoved his hands into his coat pockets. "But I'm not sure that there's much you can do for the colonel. Do you know that he's very sick?"

She managed to nod her head. "He has a cancer and the doctor says that he's dying."

"I'm sorry."

"So am I." Katherine expelled a deep breath. "All my life Father has been a tower of strength and integrity. He's shattered, and I mean to be his strength now."

"But where will you sleep and what will you eat?"

"I'll sleep on the floor beside his cot, and we'll eat with whatever money we can earn from selling papers on the streets. I mean to help him put out a good newspaper."

"And he's agreed to your help?"

"No. He thinks that I'm going to stay a few days and then go back to Denver on the next eastbound train. I see no reason to tell him my true intentions."

"Katherine, the very first thing you have to do is to try and sober him up."

"I know. I'll talk to the doctor about getting his dosage of laudanum increased. I don't see why he has to suffer so."

"Me neither."

Longarm fumbled for his money. "Here," he said, "take this and live on it until things get better."

"I can't do that."

"Take it," he insisted, grabbing her hand and shoving the money into her palm. "You need the money worse than I do."

"Thank you," she whispered. "I'm going to take care of my father and bring his newspaper back to respectability. That's what I'm going to do, Custis."

"I know."

"And you?"

"I'm going back to Anderson's in the morning and rent or buy a horse and ride up to the Comstock Lode in search of Heck Wilcox and them other two."

"And if you find them?"

"I've got some reward money they're due and some words from my boss that they need to hear."

"I hope they listen instead of wanting to fight."

"Me too," Longarm said, steeling himself, "but I'm not too damned hopeful."

"What if you have to face Heck Wilcox with a gun?"

"Then I'll do my best to wing him."

"But wouldn't that be dangerous?"

"Yeah," Longarm admitted. "Real dangerous. But that's part of the job."

Katherine reached up and kissed him on the cheek. "You know, when you toppled over onto me as the train was leaving Denver, I thought you must be the clumsiest but handsomest man I'd ever seen."

Longarm grinned. "You had the first part right."

"No, I didn't."

Longarm tipped his hat to her. "I'd best be going before I steal you away from your father. Fact of the matter is, he needs you even more than I do right now."

"We'll be fine."

As he turned and walked away, Longarm sure hoped so. He was upset that Katherine had walked into such a mess, and yet he could not really blame the colonel. Maybe the man could have been handling a fatal cancer better, but constant pain could erode even a strong man's courage. If there was one consolation, it was that Katherine would rise to the occasion and do whatever was necessary to help her father and make his dying days bearable.

## Chapter 8

In the morning, Longarm had a good but lonely breakfast, then returned to Mort Anderson's stable. The man was feeding his horses, and Longarm was anxious to buy or rent a horse and hit the trail. The sooner he caught up with Heck Wilcox and the others, the sooner he'd be able to return and help Katherine and her dying father.

"I might be looking to buy a good horse," Longarm began, for he had often found that an eager buyer is the one that gets stung. "Or rent one."

"How long you going to be needing an animal?"

"I don't know," Longarm said. "The truth of the matter is that I have to find Heck Wilcox and his two friends. If they're on the Comstock as you suggested, I'll only need a horse for a couple of days."

"Probably they won't be on the Comstock."

"But you said you thought they might be."

"Well, I heard they were," Anderson said. "But don't forget, those fellas are bounty hunters. In that business, you never stop for very long."

"True," Longarm said. "Show me the horses you have for rent and for sale."

"Got a couple of good ones. How much is the government willin' to spend?"

"Up to fifty dollars, but you'd have to throw in a saddle, bridle, and blanket."

Anderson stopped in his tracks. "Well, hell's fire! I haven't got any horses and outfits that cheap. Not unless you want an old broken-down kid's horse."

"Show me what you have," Longarm ordered. "Maybe the government can go a little higher."

"They better go a lot higher if you want to buy a good saddle horse. I guarantee every horse for sound legs and wind. I don't sell kickers, buckers, or biters. You get a horse from me, Marshal, you know you're buyin' nothing but the very best. Why, all the Nevada senators and state assemblymen buy their horses right here at this livery. And so does our esteemed governor."

"Quit the sales pitch and show me some good horseflesh, Mort. I'm in a hurry."

Anderson led Longarm outside and behind the barn, where he had a number of pole corrals containing a couple dozen horses.

Hooking his boot heel over a lower rail, Anderson said, "That buckskin is a real corker, Marshal. I know he's fast and strong. How's he look to you?"

"Too steep in the pasterns," Longarm said. "He'd be rougher than a cob to ride. Probably splinter a man's tailbone at the trot."

"Then what do you think of that palomino?"

"He's a loafer," Longarm judged. "Looks lazy as a sloth. I'd probably have to whip his hide off him to make him gallop."

"And the appaloosa?"

"Jug-headed and stubborn from the looks of him."

"You are mighty damn picky for a man with little money to spend."

"Maybe I'll just take the Virginia & Truckee Railroad up to the Comstock," Longarm said, liking the looks of a sorrel gelding in the next pen but not letting Anderson see his interest. "If I don't find Heck up there, I can always buy a horse in Virginia City or Gold Hill."

"Why, you'd pay double my price! Hay is twice as much up there 'cause it costs so much to haul up the grade. You'll get stung real bad if you try to buy a decent riding horse up on the Comstock Lode."

Longarm knew this to be the truth, for he'd once tried to buy a horse from a stable in Virginia City and had been appalled at the asking price. He strolled over to the next pen and still avoided looking at the handsome sorrel gelding. "What about that bay mare?"

"She's a good mare. Got a little age on her."

"How old?"

Anderson shrugged. "She's a smooth mouth so it's hard to say. But from the way her teeth are parroting out, I'd guess she's around sixteen."

"That is a little too old for the hard riding that I might have to do if I need to track down Wilcox, Berry, and Denton."

"I'd say you need the best horse you can find," Anderson offered. "Now that sorrel gelding is a real handsome bugger, ain't he, though?"

"He's a little small for a man my size."

"Small! Why, he's near sixteen hands!"

"Naw. Probably not much over fifteen. Light in the front quarters too. Probably don't have a lot of lung power."

"Hell, Marshal! He's a runnin' fool! And while he is a little light, he'll still go about eleven hundred pounds. You grain him and—"

"Grain him?" Longarm laughed. "Mr. Anderson, I need a horse that can live off sagebrush and outrun a jackrabbit."

"He's the best I've got. Wouldn't take less than a hundred dollars for that horse."

"Sixty."

"Ninety."

"Eighty and you throw in a good outfit and a sack of grain."

"Eighty-five and you've got the finest-grade horse in northern Nevada. One that will carry you out of a bad fix, in the unlikely but possible event that you run into a buzz saw when you find them three ex-marshals."

"It's a deal, if you put a fresh pair of shoes on him and have him grained and ready to ride in two hours."

"A deal, if you got cash on the barrel head."

"I do."

Anderson stuck out his dirty and calloused hand. "You skinned me, Marshal. But I always like to do a public service and help out a lawman."

"Sure you do," Longarm said, believing that quite the opposite was true.

Longarm left Anderson's Livery and went to talk to the sheriff. After hearing Mort speak of the man, Longarm didn't have much hope that Sheriff Wilbur was going to be of any assistance. It was a pathetic thing when a frightened sheriff ran out on the very town he'd sworn to protect.

Sheriff Bert Wilbur turned out to be a slovenly man in his mid-thirties. When Longarm walked into his office, the man was leaning back in his desk chair with his feet up and his hat tipped over his unshaven face. He was snoring loudly and before Longarm woke him up, he had a good look around.

The office was a rat's nest. The desk where Wilbur's feet rested was covered with old newspapers, wanted posters, and a few dime novels whose cheap covers depicted daring shootouts. There were dirty dishes and the remains of unfinished meals stacked here and there, some on the floor. The rifle rack was broken and hung lopsided on the wall, and the cell in the back wasn't fit for a pig, much less a human being.

"What a slob," Longarm muttered, wondering how on earth this sorry excuse for a sheriff had ever gotten himself elected into office.

Longarm walked over to the man and batted his boots off the desk. "Wake up, Wilbur!"

The sheriff started so badly that he almost flipped over backward in his swivel chair. When his boots struck the floor, he reared back and his hand stabbed ineffectually for his six-gun, but the gun was wedged between himself and the chair so tightly he couldn't pull it free.

"Hold up there," Longarm drawled, pulling his badge out of his pocket. "I'm a federal officer. Deputy Marshal Custis Long working out of Denver."

Wilbur's struggles ceased. "Jezus! Can't you just wake a man up politely instead of scarin' the crap right outa him?"

"Why are you sleeping?" Longarm asked. "It's only ten o'clock in the morning."

"I have to stay up half the night to keep order in the saloons," Wilbur said, tearing his eyes from Longarm's shiny federal officer's badge. "Sometimes I don't get to sleep at all."

"What happened last night?"

"Nothin', but I'm savin' up for a bad one."

Longarm swore under his breath. He'd seen a lot of pathetic sheriffs and town marshals, but this man easily took the prize for being the worst.

"I was sent here to find Heck Wilcox, Jim Denton, and Bill Berry. I understand that they captured One-Eared George and a couple of his men."

"Captured? Ha! They found and killed 'em! Beat 'em plumb to death, then cut George's damned ear off!"

"I know," Longarm said. "We got it in Denver and a note asking for a three-hundred-dollar reward."

"Our governor is fit to be tied about that. One-Eared George wasn't much, but he didn't deserve to be beat to death and neither did his boys. They was on the level of chicken thieves, at least around here. Only problem is, they stole the *governor's* chickens!"

When Longarm looked as if he didn't believe it, Sheriff Wilbur bounced to his feet. "It's the truth! They got drunk as loons and they must have gone after the governor's chickens on a damned dare. Anyway, they hauled them chickens down to the saloons and tried to auction 'em off! It was the damnedest joke ever played on the governor and the chickens brought about five dollars each!"

Wilbur guffawed heartily until Longarm said, "Are you finished?"

Wilbur's laugh trickled into a weak grin. "Sure."

"I understand that your governor decided to pardon One-Eared George and his two accomplices."

"That's right. But only after they gave him the money they'd earned from the chicken auction. Governor was happy then because he said the chickens wasn't even good layers. You can read all about it in some old issues of the *Carson Courier* that I've got layin' around here someplace. Why, the editor had hisself quite a field day writin' about it."

"I'm sure that he did," Longarm said, watching as the sheriff began to mull through some old food-stained issues of the newspaper. "But never mind that. Where is Heck Wilcox and the two others right now?"

"In Hell, I hope."

"And if they're not in Hell?"

"I heard they was going to try and catch stagecoach robbers that have a state reward on their heads. I got their reward poster around here someplace."

Longarm saw Wilbur cast a doleful look around at his walls where some old yellowed posters were tacked up.

"It's around here someplace."

"Forget it," Longarm said. "What was the leader's name and how much is the reward?"

"I think his name is Wade Quick, though I doubt that's his real name. He and his men have ambushed and killed four or five stagecoach drivers and shotgun guards. He has two brothers and the reward was a hundred dollars each—dead or alive."

"And they're thought to be hiding on the Comstock Lode?"

"Yeah. Last I heard."

"Thanks," Longarm said, wanting to be rid of this sorry excuse for a lawman.

"Hey, wait! Are you after them men for the reward too?"

"No."

"Then what's this all about? I'm the law here. I need to know these things."

"You don't even want to know. I hope you go back to sleep until the next election, when someone tosses you out of this filthy office."

"Well, dammit anyway!" Wilbur howled. "I try to be cooperative and help you out, and what do I get? Nothin' but insults! That sure ain't no way to treat a fellow law officer."

"You're a disgrace to my profession," Longarm said as he walked out the door.

On the way back to the livery, he stopped and bought a few supplies for the ride up to the Comstock Lode. He still had some old friends up there, and if it had not been for the trouble that awaited, he would have actually been looking forward to the trip.

Fifteen minutes later, Longarm rode out of Carson City despite a powerful urge to stop and visit with Katherine Chambers. But he finally decided that the easiest and wisest thing to do was to steer clear of Katherine for a while and let her handle things on her own. He'd see her when he returned to Carson City.

If he lived to return.

# Chapter 9

Longarm rode east out of Carson City into the low, barren hills as he paralleled the course of the meandering Carson River. His new sorrel gelding proved to be as eager a traveler as he'd expected, and it felt good to be back in the saddle again. Because Longarm traveled so extensively, there was little point in owning a horse of his own, but when he bought an especially good one like this sorrel, he always thought about having it shipped back to Denver.

The day was bright and breezy, with wispy clouds scudding across an azure sky. Ten years earlier the Carson River had been clogged with timber mills, but now they were all gone and young cottonwoods were starting to replace the thousands that had been chopped down for fuel or mine timbering.

After several hours of pleasant riding Longarm entered Gold Canyon and began the steep climb that brought him to Silver City. He could see that the mining town was in a sharp decline. Its once-great ore-stamping mills were now mostly closed, and the traffic up the canyon was a mere trickle compared to the torrent that had surged up and down Gold Canyon during the booming years when the lure of Comstock gold brought miners and speculators from around the world. But now, most of the saloons and businesses were either boarded up or simply abandoned.

When Longarm approached a narrow defile between two towering pillars of rock called Devil's Gate, two disreputable-looking men in big dirty overalls stepped out to block his path. They each carried shotguns and looked mean-spirited. Longarm knew trouble when it stepped into his path, and he shifted his right hand to his saddlehorn where it would be near the butt of his six-gun.

"Be two bits fer you, two bits for your horse to pass through our gate," one of the men said, spitting a stream of tobacco juice between the sorrel's feet.

Longarm thumbed his Stetson back and gazed upward. He didn't see anyone standing above with a loaded weapon, and the idea of having to pay these two characters was galling. This was a county road, free for anyone to travel.

"Well?" the second man said. "Are you comin' through our property, or not?"

"I don't think it's your property," Longarm said. "In fact, I *know* that this is a public road. So I think that you had both best step aside."

One of the men inched his shotgun upward a little and his message was clear and ominous. "I think you'd better come up with the coin or else turn that handsome sorrel ride around and ride back to wherever you came from."

"And if I don't?"

"That's a mighty nice horse. Clyde and I could probably get seventy or eight dollars for him."

"That's what I thought you'd say."

"I figured you'd see it our way," Clyde crowed. "It ain't worth gettin' shot over four bits."

"You're right," Longarm said, right hand snaking off his saddlehorn to whip out his Colt. He cocked it in one smooth motion, leveled it between the pair, and said, "You boys have a choice to make. Drop the shotguns or I'll drop you."

Clyde was a fool. His shotgun jerked up and Longarm pulled the trigger, his slug striking the man in the leg, just above the knee. Clyde screamed and grabbed his leg, shotgun tumbling to the ground. The second man froze, paralyzed by fear and indecision.

"Please, don't shoot me! I got a mother!"

"We all have mothers," Longarm snapped.

"But mine is hungry!"

"I could use a shotgun and you could use a new profession. How much?"

The man looked down at the shotgun hanging in his fist. "I paid ten dollars for it."

Longarm dismounted, Colt still in his hand. He went over to the wounded man and studied the work of his bullet. "You're going to live, quit howling."

"But it hurts and I'm bleeding to death!"

"No, you're not," Longarm said. "Take off your shirt."

Clyde's eyes grew round. "You gun me down and now you're going to steal the shirt off my damned back!"

"Hell, no! I'm going to tear it into strips for bandaging and tie up that leg."

Clyde sobbed, but he did as Longarm ordered. When the leg was bandaged, Clyde whimpered, "Now I got to go and pay a doc five or ten dollars to dig this slug outa my leg!"

"Yep."

"But I ain't got that much money!"

Longarm was disgusted. He tore the shotgun out of the other man's fists and checked to make sure that it was in good working condition. Satisfied, he dug ten dollars out of his pants pocket and gave it to the wounded man. "Here, this ought to pay for the doc."

"But that's *my* money!" the other man said.

"He borrowed it," Longarm snapped, jamming a boot into his stirrup and swinging onto the sorrel.

The two men swore in helpless fury, but Longarm didn't care. He'd seen a mean streak in both of them. "Clyde, if you're still here when I come back through, I'll shoot your other leg with this shotgun."

"But how am I gonna feed Mamma?"

"Beats the hell outa me," Longarm said. "But I wouldn't advise trying to hold up a bank or some stupid thing like that. You'd get yourselves killed for certain."

Near the top of the canyon rested Gold Hill, once a rival to the famed Virginia City. Longarm remembered drinking green beer from a local brewery and how the painted ladies had flocked to the mining yards on payday. But now, only a few mines were operating and the rest had closed, leaving gaping holes in the hillsides and mountainous piles of ore tailings as silent monuments to their passing.

The last quarter of a mile to the top was a very steep climb, and even the young and strong sorrel was humping and puffing by the time he crossed over the Divide. Longarm dismounted, loosed his cinch, and let the animal blow for a few minutes while he gazed out what had been known around the world as "The Queen of the Comstock." In its heyday, Virginia City had boasted a population of over thirty thousand intrepid souls. Now, with production falling, Longarm supposed that there were less than five thousand people remaining on the Comstock.

Still, five thousand was a big city by frontier standards, and the streets were busy with wagons, horsemen, and pedestrians. The Fourth Ward School remained in operation, and several of the larger mines were still working, as evidenced by their smokestacks fed by mighty steam engines that hoisted men, supplies, and ore out of the belly of Sun Mountain.

"You got your second wind yet?" Longarm asked.

When the sorrel nuzzled him, Longarm scratched it behind the ears and retightened his cinch. He mounted the horse to ride on up C Street past the firehouse, the struggling saloons, and the famed *Territorial Enterprise*, where a couple of gifted writers with pen names like Mark Twain and Dan de Quille had won admiration and fame.

Longarm passed the Silver Dollar and the Delta saloons, and drew rein at the Bucket of Blood Saloon. It had a long mahogany bar and huge glass window, where a man could drink good beer and gaze out across an endless ocean of Nevada hills. Longarm dismounted and went inside, suddenly thirsty and eager to see a friendly and familiar face.

"Marshal Long!" the bartender shouted with obvious delight. "If you ain't a sight for sore eyes!"

"How you doin', Pete?"

"Just fine, now that you've walked in."

Longarm saw that there were only four other customers besides himself. He could remember when a man would have to wait twenty minutes to get near enough to the bar to order his drink. Things had really changed.

"Beer or whiskey?"

"I'll have beer," Longarm said.

"All right, but it isn't as good as you're used to havin' here. Our last brewery shut down and moved to California. What we get now isn't top grade and it costs a little more because of the freighting charges."

"It'll be fine, Pete. The company is still the best."

The bartender liked that remark. Pete Dowd was a pleasant Irishman who enjoyed conversation, especially when it was with someone who had come from beyond the Comstock and could tell him about national affairs.

"I'm sorry things are so slow," Longarm said. "Half the businesses are boarded up."

"Yeah, but the Meteorite Mine hit a new vein of silver at twelve hundred feet last week and it's causing quite a stir. They hired on sixty miners and everyone is hoping that it is going to turn things around. News travels fast and we're seeing new men arriving every day asking for work."

"Well," Longarm said, "I sure hope that they find it. It'd be a shame to see Virginia City turn into a ghost town."

"Damn right it would." Pete poured them both glasses of frothy beer. "But I ain't givin' up and neither are my neighbors. We're bettin' on a comeback. Another big strike. Maybe bigger than ever."

"Let's drink to that," Longarm said, raising his glass.

They drank deeply. "You're right, Pete. Your beer isn't as good as it used to be."

"Is anything as we get older?"

Longarm chuckled. "No, I guess not. Tell me, is Heck Wilcox, Bill Berry, or Jim Denton in town?"

"I think Berry might be," Pete said, brow furrowing with concern. "He comes in every few days. Seems to be at loose ends and he can be pretty surly. I just fill his glass and leave him alone."

"I see. And the others?"

"Old Heck has gone off somewhere to raise hell and everyone is enjoying the peace. I don't know about Jim Denton. He could be most anywhere."

"I understand that they're in the bounty-hunting business," Longarm said matter-of-factly.

"That's what they say. I used to see them together all the time when they were federal marshals. But after they quit and then beat One-Eared George and his friends to death, they drifted apart."

"Exactly what happened with One-Eared?"

"From what I've been told, Heck, Jim, and Bill found him and his buddies hiding in an abandoned mine down in Silver City. I guess they thought that there was some hidden gold or cash and tried to make them thieves talk. When One-Eared claimed that there wasn't, he and his friends were beaten to death because they wouldn't talk."

"That sure isn't the Heck Wilcox I knew," Longarm said, draining his glass. "It just doesn't fit."

"Heck changed, Custis. Age didn't become him like it does some men. Heck got ornery and short-tempered. He started drinking too much for his own good, and it got so that my saloon would actually clear out when he came in to drink."

"Damn," Longarm muttered. "Give me another beer."

When Pete refilled his glass, the bartender continued. "Heck and his boys started to running roughshod over folks. They came in here one day about half drunk and said that they would 'protect' my establishment from the rougher element in town. Can you imagine? I've been here almost twenty years and I never paid no one for protection! I was galled."

"And you refused?"

"Of course! Next night, Heck came in drunk and started a brawl. Broke the place up. Tables, chairs. I was scared they were going to come over the bar and bust up my bottles and mirror. I pulled a shotgun out and fired one barrel into the ceiling."

Pete pointed upward. "You can see where my ceiling is all chewed up."

Longarm craned his head back. "Yeah, I can see."

"It broke up the fight. Heck cussed me out and left. I knew he'd started the fight so I'd change my mind and pay him and his friends protection money."

"So what happened then?"

"Heck disappeared a few weeks later. Jim shows up every few weeks, and Bill Berry is living up here someplace. Last I heard, he was still in the 'protection' business, when he wasn't trying to collect a bounty."

"I see." Longarm found a cheroot and bit off its tip, then spit it into the sawdust at his feet. "But you don't know where Bill Berry is staying?"

"Nope. But he should be easy to find."

"I'll go see the sheriff."

"I'm afraid that we don't have one anymore."

"Shot?"

"Run off by Heck a couple of months back. And the city council was so disgusted that they decided not to replace him. They figured there wasn't much use in payin' a sheriff in the good times when he wouldn't stand up and show some backbone during the bad times."

"That makes sense," Longarm said. "So who would you think I should ask about Berry?"

"Try askin' a woman who works over at the Silver Queen. Her name is Liz. She's got blond hair and a scar on her right cheek, but she's still pretty. Liz and Berry were sweet on each other awhile back. Liz is pretty tough, but she's generally honest. Besides, if Berry did her wrong, she just might want to see you catch up with him."

"I'll go see her right now," Longarm decided, finishing his beer.

"Come on back when you can!" Pete yelled. "Next beer is on the house!"

Longarm walked out of the Bucket of Blood Saloon and across the street. The Silver Queen's main attraction was the "Silver Queen" herself, a fifteen-foot-tall painting of a beautiful Western belle who wore a gown adorned with over three thousand silver dollars. The dress, with its wide belt of twenty-dollar gold pieces, was worth a small fortune.

Longarm had never felt relaxed in the Silver Queen, but he'd shared a few drinks there over the years and knew the bartender by name. "How you doin', Gus?"

"Why, if it ain't Marshal Custis Long! How about a drink on the house?"

"Sure. Make it beer."

"Whatever you say, Marshal. It's been a while since we've seen you."

"About eight months. I'm looking for Liz. I understand that she works here."

Gus poured the beer, slid it across the bar, and said, "She was working here until two days ago."

"Oh?"

"Yeah. She just upped and quit."

"Any idea why?"

"I think she went to live with Bill Berry. Said something about him having a chance to earn a big bounty."

"Where can I find them?"

"Last I heard, Berry lived in a small shack up on A Street. But I wouldn't swear by that. Has Berry done something wrong?"

"I've got some reward money for him," Longarm said, deciding not to also mention that he was sent to warn the man that further embarrassments as a bounty hunter would not be appreciated or even tolerated.

"Well, Berry will be glad to see you! And now that I think about it, I'm almost sure that the man is living on A Street. Go up Taylor, then turn right on A Street and you'll see his house. It's got a dead cottonwood tree in the front and a picket fence with the gate hanging on one hinge."

Longarm nodded. He realized that Gus had known exactly where to find Berry, but wasn't going to say until he knew Longarm's intentions. The promise of a reward was enough to get him to talk.

"Thanks for the beer," Longarm said.

"Don't mention it! Come on back and tell Berry to do the same and to bring that reward money!"

Longarm had no trouble locating Berry's house. By the time he arrived, it was dusk and there were no lights on inside, but the door was ajar.

"Anybody home? Bill, it's Custis Long! We need to talk! I got some money for you!"

No answer.

Longarm shrugged. He toed open the door and groped into the dim interior, striking a match with his thumbnail. Suddenly, Longarm reached for his six-gun as his eyes locked onto the body of a pretty young woman with a bowie knife embedded in her chest.

# Chapter 10

The undertaker waited patiently until Longarm was through with the doctor. Then he shuffled forward, piously wringing his hands. "Marshal, to my knowledge, Miss Alcott had no relatives. Even so, I'm sure that you'll want to see that the poor woman is honored with a first-class funeral."

"Take up a collection," Longarm said, digging five dollars out of his pockets. "Here, you can start it with this."

The undertaker did not reach for the money. "Marshal, I beg your pardon, but I'm afraid that taking up a collection is not a service that I provide."

"Then give the money to Gus and ask him to do it for you," Longarm said tightly. "But either way, this woman gets a good burial with a nice casket and flowers. Is that clearly understood?"

The undertaker, a cadaverous-looking man with a shock of wild hair and the smell of whiskey on him, nodded his head. "I'll see that she is well taken care of, you can rest assured."

"Good."

Longarm turned back to the doctor and ushered the man out into the street. "Doc, have you heard of a place called Whiskeyville?"

"I sure have. It's a little boom town about sixty miles southeast of here. Why do you ask?"

"There was a burned letter in the stove. I tried to pick it out but it disintegrated. Then I found its envelope and it was postmarked Whiskeyville."

"So?"

"It was addressed to Bill Berry and the initials JD were at the top of the envelope. I take that to mean Jim Denton."

"That's likely. But so what?"

"Well," Longarm said, "there isn't much doubt that it was Bill who stabbed Liz to death. I recognized his bowie knife. Furthermore, it seems to me that the letter from Jim Denton might have something to do with going after a bounty on the heads of a stagecoach robber named Wade Quick and his brothers."

"Sure, I've heard of them. They hit a stage in Silver City only three weeks ago and shot the driver to pieces. But aren't you reaching for straws?"

"It's the only lead I have," Longarm confessed. "Besides, I have to find Denton, and I feel pretty sure that Whiskeyville is as good a starting point as any."

The doctor looked down at the dead woman. "I liked Liz," he said. "She was rough, but honest and fun-loving. She was just attracted by the wrong kind of man."

"That happens," Longarm said.

"But the thing that amazes me," the doctor said, "is that Berry didn't even try to hide her body. You'd think that the last thing he'd want is to be tied to a murder."

"Yeah, unless he isn't planning on coming back."

Longarm drew a cheroot and jammed it into the corner of his mouth without bothering to light it. "You see, Bill Berry understands the limits of the law."

"What does that mean?"

"It means he doesn't fear it because he knows he can change his name and move away."

"But why kill Miss Alcott?"

"I don't know," Longarm admitted. "I've been a federal marshal for a lot of years and I've seen dozens of women killed in fits of passion. Maybe Berry will tell me, but I doubt it."

"Without a witness, can he even be charged with murder and brought to trial?"

"Yes, but it won't come to that."

The doctor started to ask why, but when he looked into Longarm's eyes, he changed his mind. "Well," he said quietly, "if you need any testimony as to cause of death, I'll be happy to cooperate."

"It would be appreciated," Longarm said. "I'll be leaving for Whiskeyville at first light. In the meantime, I'm still trying to get a lead on Heck Wilcox."

"Did you talk to old Caleb down at the gun store?"

"No."

"You should. Caleb is quite a character. I'd say that he was about the only man in Virginia City that Heck Wilcox treated with any kind of respect. They're both ornery old badgers. Caleb and Heck used to like to sit on the boardwalk all afternoon and swap lies and a bottle of rye whiskey."

"I'll speak to Caleb," Longarm said hopefully. "Thanks for the tip."

"You better not thank me until after you've met Caleb. He's one of the best liars I've ever heard and you can't believe a word he'll tell you. I really don't know if you'll gain from speaking to a man like that."

"Sometimes you can learn more by listening to what those old fellas *don't* say," Longarm drawled.

He took one last look at the body, and then he patted his coat pocket to make sure that the murder weapon was still in his possession. It was going to be real interesting to see Bill Berry's expression when he handed him the knife with its blade crusted with Liz Alcott's dried blood. After that, there might be hell to pay.

It was easy enough to find Caleb the gunsmith. The old man was working on a nice .45-caliber Smith & Wesson revolver when Longarm walked into his cluttered little shop. Caleb was bent over a workbench and intent on fixing the revolver. Longarm did not want to disturb him. Instead, he examined a rack of rifles, and found a beautiful Winchester Model '73 that looked almost new and that he thought would be a wonderful complement to the shotgun he'd purchased at Devil's Gate.

"What do you want?" Caleb finally said after Longarm had thoroughly inspected the Winchester.

"How much for this one?"

"Sixty dollars."

Longarm smiled. "Unless you have eyes in the back of your head, how do you know which rifle I'm talking about?"

"I can tell by the sound of the action. It's the Winchester '73 and the price is sixty dollars. Don't matter to me if you buy it or not."

"You're one hell of a salesman," Longarm said cryptically. "I'll take the rifle."

"Leave your money on the counter and get outa here."

Longarm used Bill Berry's share of the reward money because the man wasn't going to need it anyway. Either Bill was going to prison for murdering Liz, or he was going to be hanged. Longarm slapped sixty dollars down on the counter.

"Don't you want to count it?"

"Nope."

"I need some ammunition."

"You kin buy 'em at the general store."

Longarm shouldered the handsome Winchester. "Old man, I generally like to face someone that I'm doing business with, so turn around or the first thing I'm going to do with this rifle is to put a big goose egg on the back of your ugly head."

Caleb finally turned around. He was missing one eye and didn't bother to wear an eye patch. There was a sabre slash across that empty eye that furrowed deeply all the way down across his jaw. Whoever had sutured the wound had done a terrible job. Longarm guessed Caleb had received his sabre slash during the Civil War, most likely during one of the major battles, when entire limb amputations had been done in less than ten minutes due to the number of wounded and dying soldiers.

"Who the hell are you?"

"I'm Deputy Marshal Custis Long. I'm Heck Wilcox's friend and I'm looking for him."

The gunsmith's empty eye socket twitched as he recognized the name. "Yeah, Heck told me about you. Sometimes when he got real drunk, he'd say you were like a son."

"Heck and I have ridden some long trails together. The truth is that I owe that man my life several times over."

"He claimed you also saved his hide a time or two. Used to talk about that fight you had with the McLarin brothers over in Cheyenne. Said that you both stood up against five of them bastards and gunned 'em all down in the street."

"They were drunk and figured that Heck and I were bluffing. But we weren't."

"So what do you want to know?"

"Where is Heck?"

Caleb shrugged his thin, bent shoulders. "I don't know."

"Why did he give up his badge?"

"Bounty money is pretty good."

"So was his job," Longarm said bluntly. "Heck was his own boss. He'd been with the agency almost twenty years. He was well respected."

"And broke."

"He'd have been broke even if he'd inherited a fortune every year," Longarm said pointedly. "Heck spent money like it was dirt. He never even cared about money. Now everyone is trying to tell me that suddenly he became greedy. I don't buy it. You don't change a man's character as easy as a pair of dirty socks."

"Did you know that Heck has a daughter?"

Longarm blinked. "No."

"Well, he didn't either. But there was this gal come

by to see him and her name was Irma. Irma said that they had a daughter together and that she was in some kind of big trouble."

"What kind of trouble?"

"I don't know," Caleb said. "But after she left, Heck got drunk for two weeks straight. Next thing I know, he's hooked up with Bill Berry and Jim Denton and they're no longer marshals. They're goddamn bounty hunters."

Longarm frowned. "Do you know where this Irma came from or where she is now?"

"She left the next day on a stage heading south."

"No last name?"

"Nothing." Caleb scowled. "She was a dance-hall woman but past her prime. I had the feeling that she'd been real pretty about ten years ago. Anyway, she sure changed Heck. He wasn't himself after that. Next thing I know, he's ridin' off to catch a gang of outlaws for their reward money."

"One-Eared George and his gang?"

"Yeah."

"And you think Heck is doing all this because he suddenly found out he had a daughter?"

"Sure!" Caleb exclaimed. "Why else would he give up his badge and a job he liked? He was proud of being a United States marshal."

"That's what I always thought. But then he sent in One-Eared George's only ear to our federal office in Denver asking for the reward. Included was his badge. That isn't like Heck."

The gunsmith frowned. "You got a seegar?"

"Sure," Longarm answered, taking two out, giving one to Caleb and then lighting them both up before saying, "Look, Caleb, I got to find Heck before he gets afoul of the law—if he isn't already."

"And then what are you going to do?"

"Depends on him," Longarm said. "Maybe I'm the only one that can talk some sense into that pig-headed old bastard. Maybe he'll listen close to me before he gets sent to prison or the gallows."

"Heck wouldn't let anyone send him to prison or to a hangman," Caleb said. "He'd rather go down fighting, even against a man that he thought of as a son."

Longarm didn't want to admit it to himself, but he thought that Caleb was probably right. "Do you think this Irma woman might have come from a place called Whiskeyville?"

"Why you ask?"

"Because that's where I think I'm going to find Bill Berry. He murdered Liz Alcott from the Silver Queen and ran. My guess is that is where he's headed."

"I wouldn't know about that. But I do know one thing."

"What's that?"

"Berry and Denton are two bad apples. Old Heck ought to see that, but he don't. He told me that they were in this bounty-huntin' thing together. He said that they were both damn good fighters and the kind he wanted to have when he got into a tight fix."

"Bill Berry is a woman-killer," Longarm said with contempt. "He's not the kind of man you'd want to turn your back on."

"I know that," Caleb said. "You know that. But old Heck don't seem to know that."

"That's why I've got to find him in a hurry," Longarm said, turning on his heel and starting for the door.

"Hey!"

Longarm turned just in time to catch a box of shells for his new Winchester. Caleb grinned, his smile twisted by the sabre scar. Longarm nodded with appreciation. "Thanks."

"You save that old man's ass and drag it back here!" Caleb called. "He's good with guns and he's good to drink rye whiskey with in the afternoon."

"I know," Longarm said as he went out the door.

# Chapter 11

Longarm rode from sunup until just after sundown to reach Whiskeyville. The boom town was situated in a long, narrow valley choked with sage and surrounded by high, barren hills. There were two big mines, the Condor and the Thunder, and both employed over a hundred men. The town itself wasn't much, mostly clapboard buildings with impressive facades and a sea of canvas tents. Those miners unable to afford to rent bunk space in a shack or tent were living in caves and holes they'd dug into the earth and then covered with a tarp.

Whiskeyville boasted six saloons, all of them crowded. At the west end of the town there was a red, barn-sized whorehouse called the Cat Corral. It even had a porch where its girls could lounge about in rocking chairs whistling and bantering with the passersby and generating good-natured laughter and a steady stream of business.

Whiskeyville was the kind of a place where life was cheap and the liquor was even worse than the women.

"Evening!" a liveryman called when Longarm rode into his yard. "You and your horse both look plumb played out."

"We are," Longarm said wearily. "We rode down from Virginia City."

"That's a two-day ride for most. You got a fine little horse, mister."

"I know that. How much to feed and double-grain him?"

"About six bits a day. You see, I got to have all my hay and grain hauled in from the Carson Valley. I'm tellin' you, that ain't cheap."

"Fine." Longarm paid the man for two days' board. "Will you lock up my rifle and outfit?"

"Yep. I'll put 'em under lock and key for an extra two bits."

"You got it," Longarm said. "I'm looking for a man named Bill Berry."

"Sorry, don't ring a bell. What's he look like?"

"About my height. Black hair and black mustache. Fancy dresser. He shaves every day and he polishes his boots."

"Ain't seen no polished boots in Whiskeyville. But if'n I was you and lookin' for a ladies' man, first place I'd visit is the Cat Corral."

"Good idea."

Longarm took his shotgun and set out down the street to look for Bill Berry. The whorehouses in these boom towns were generally little more than fancy cribs, the kind he'd seen in the back streets of Cheyenne and the other hell-on-wheels railroad towns that had mushroomed up so fast during the construction of the transcontinental railroad. In Whiskeyville, the Cat Corral was painted red and sat boldly in the center of town. At the moment the girls were all inside.

Outside, the Cat Corral was guarded by a big man who stepped into Longarm's path. "Nobody goes in unless they leave their weapons outside, mister. House rules."

Longarm reached into his pocket and flashed his badge. "This is official business."

"Sure it is, Marshal," the guard said with a smirk. "I reckon you can go in armed since you're the law."

"Wise decision on your part."

The "house" was nothing more or less than a dingy cavern of sex and sin partitioned into a dozen stalls, one for each of the girls. Each stall had a door that could be closed for privacy, and was enclosed by little walls only about six feet high. It was dim inside the Cat Corral, and Longarm thought the place should have been called the Cat Box. The moment that he entered, several girls who were not already entertaining men came outside their stalls and sashayed forward, hips moving provocatively as they judged Longarm for the amount of money he carried.

"Hello, ladies," Longarm said, flashing his badge.

The women underwent an immediate and dramatic transformation. Their painted, brittle smiles melted and they drew back with suspicion.

"What do you want?" said one.

"I'm looking for a man."

"Then you're in the wrong place. We're all women."

The women laughed, and one made an obscene bumping gesture with her hips which Longarm chose to ignore. "I'm looking for a man who stabbed a woman to death in Virginia City a few days ago."

The women exchanged glances and their personalities seemed to undergo another marked change, this time for the better. A large blonde with bright red lipstick and thick powder on her cheeks asked, "Was she one of us?"

"Yeah," Longarm said. "She worked in a saloon, but she worked outside too. Nice woman that damn sure didn't deserve to die. I think the man that killed her is in Whiskeyville."

"What's his name?" a little brunette asked.

"Bill Berry."

The girls all shook their heads. "Never heard of him."

"I expect he changed his name," Longarm said, and then went on to describe the man just he'd done for Caleb.

"I know him!" A plump, washed-out-looking blonde with an enormous bust said, looking quite proud of herself. "He's a dandy, all right."

"What's he calling himself now?"

"Bob Berryman."

Longarm had to smile at that. "Not very imaginative, is he? Where'd you see him last?"

"In that little room to your right, Marshal." She winked. "Can I show you?"

The other girls hooted and Longarm chuckled. "I'd like that, but maybe some other time. Any idea where Berry is now?"

"Nope. He didn't come for talk, I'll tell you. Fact is, he didn't say much to me at all but just had his pleasure. I asked him his name and—come to think of it—he sort of hesitated, like he didn't even know it. I smiled, and that's when he said Bob Berryman. Course, I figured he had a wife or somethin' and had to make the name up."

"Oh," Longarm said, "he made it up, all right. But only because he is a murderer."

The brunette said, "What should we do if he shows up again and wants a ride?"

"Better give it to him," Longarm said. "And then try and get word to me while you keep him busy."

"Is there a reward?" the big blonde asked. "If there is, we'd as soon have it as anyone."

"I expect there will be if there isn't already," Longarm said. "But tell you what, I'll kick in twenty-five dollars just to make sure."

"Fair enough."

Longarm was propositioned several more times before he could leave, but managed to extricate himself and head off toward the saloons where he was hoping to find Berry, Denton, and maybe even Heck Wilcox.

Longarm got lucky and found Berry playing faro at the Payday Saloon. His first impulse was to draw his gun, march over to Berry, and arrest the man for the murder of Liz Alcott. But something made him hesitate. There was no sign of Jim Denton or Heck Wilcox, and maybe it would be wiser to play it close to the vest and see what he could find out from Berry about the other two ex-deputy marshals before Longarm tipped his own hand and made the arrest.

"Sure," Longarm said quietly to himself. "That makes better sense."

Longarm ordered a beer that was nothing short of awful. He pretended not to see Berry, preferring to let himself be discovered. If Berry tried to bolt and run, then Longarm knew he'd be in for a hard chase, but he figured he could keep up. And if Berry played a bluff, as if he were innocent of any wrongdoing, then maybe Longarm could gain some important information.

It took Bill Berry almost twenty minutes to notice Longarm standing alone beside the bar, sipping his bitter beer. Longarm was watching his former colleague in the back-bar mirror and when Berry first saw him, Longarm saw the shock in the man's eyes. It quickly passed, however, and Berry was called by the other players back to his game.

Longarm felt tense. If Berry thought that he was about to be arrested for murder, it was not altogether inconceivable that the former marshal would open fire. And Bill Berry was both quick and deadly.

But the man decided to test the water, and summoning up his loudest voice, he threw his cards down and shouted, "Well, as I live and breath, it's my old friend, Custis Long!"

Longarm could hardly have been expected not to hear the greeting, so he turned around with his beer in hand and forced a broad, disarming grin. "Well sonofabitch! Bill, what are *you* doing here?"

Berry came hustling over, all smiles and back slaps. "Don't tell me that Billy Vail never told you that I turned in my badge."

"You did?" Longarm let his jaw drop, but only a little. "Are you serious, Bill?"

"Hell, yes! Where you been the last couple of months?"

"I've been galloping all over eastern Nevada hunting a train robber named . . . Perkins. Homer Perkins."

"Never even heard of the man."

"Well," Longarm said, mind turning quickly, "Perkins has more aliases than good sense. Anyway, what you doing here?"

"I've become a bounty hunter."

"You don't say!"

"I do say. Haven't you heard about One-Eared George? Me, Heck Wilcox, and Jim Denton captured him and his gang. We're waiting for a reward from Denver."

"Huh. Well, you know how slow them feds move, especially when it comes to loosening their purse strings."

"I sure do. Hey, maybe you'd like to join us. There's a lot more money to be made in these parts."

"I don't know," Longarm said, pretending to be about half interested in the idea. "I'm pretty happy being a federal deputy marshal."

"Shit," Berry scoffed, "all you'll get for twenty years of risking your brisket is to keep your badge and a twenty-dollar-a-month pension. Now is that what you're waiting for?"

Longarm sipped his beer and tried to look confused, which was easy enough.

"Listen," Berry said, "I'm expecting Jim Denton in most any day now and I know that he'd like to have you join us."

"What about Heck?"

"Aw," Berry scoffed, "that old heller is off on his own hook and line someplace. We worked together too long and rubbed each other's fur the wrong way."

"It sounds like you boys did just fine getting One-Eared George. What was the reward?"

"Three hundred. But that's just for starters. We got a stagecoach-robbing gang in these parts that will pay a hundred each."

"How many are in the gang?"

Berry leaned close. "Does it matter? We can find at least ten and split the thousand dollars three ways. How's that sound to you, Custis?"

Longarm blinked with surprise as the impact of Berry's words sank in deep. The man was willing to kill innocent victims just so he could claim a hundred dollars bounty on each of them. Berry was talking blood money.

"Well? You interested?"

"Real interested," Longarm said. "When do we get started?"

"Jim is off doing a little scouting for that gang right now. It's led by a fella named Wade Quick. He's the cold-bloodedest sonofabitch you'll ever want to cross. He and his brothers just shoot the driver and shotgun guard and then they rob the stage and all the passengers. If there are any women—old, young, pretty, ugly—Quick doesn't give a damn, he'll rape 'em right in the coach. If he likes their taste, he kidnaps them. If he don't like 'em, he hands them over to his brothers and the rest of the gang to use for their rough pleasure."

"Wade sounds to me like the kind of a man that needs to have his neck stretched *muy pronto*."

"He is, Custis. Now, when you're a deputy marshal and working for the government, you have to obey the laws. You're supposed to try to bring outlaws like Wade Quick and his brothers in for a trial. But if you're a bounty hunter, you just look at the wanted poster and hope that it says the reward is paid for your man alive or dead."

"I see what you're driving at."

"You can make more money in one day as a bounty hunter than you could make in six months working for Billy Vail and that bunch of bureaucrats. It's safer too. You don't have to worry about your prisoner getting the drop on you."

"Because he's dead, right?"

Bill Berry guffawed. "Right! Are you with us?"

"Damn right I am."

"Bartender," Berry shouted. "Bartender, get us some *real* beer and a bottle of whiskey to chase it down!"

"Yes, sir!" the bartender called. "Comin' right up."

Longarm drank Bill Berry's liquor and laughed at his jokes. He made fun of his own badge and profession, and lamented about how bad it was to work for Billy Vail and to draw an honest lawman's wages. He did all those things until well after midnight, and then he excused himself and went back to the livery and found a place to bed down for the night.

He fell asleep thinking of Bill Berry and Jim Denton and old Heck Wilcox. Thank God that Heck wasn't still riding with these rotten bastards!

Just before Longarm drifted off to sleep, wondering what tomorrow would bring, he thought about Katherine Chambers, and that eased his mind because she was good and honest. He really missed her, and could hardly wait to return to Carson City and feel her warm embrace before they made passionate love again.

## Chapter 12

"There!" Katherine said to her father. "It's done. One hundred copies and every page a literary masterpiece."

Colonel Ezra Chambers snorted. "Hellfire, girl! I don't know why you've been killing yourself trying to get this newspaper out on time. And a hundred copies! I tell you, Katherine, we'll be lucky to sell twenty-five after the way you fired all my stringers."

"Stringers? Why, those people were terrible writers. If they desire to write a slew of gossipy, insipid letters, then they should feel to do so in private. Father, we're a newspaper, not a gossip sheet."

"Gossip is what sells in a small town."

"But also the *news*! Why, we've got all the latest information about that new dam that the legislature wants to build. And what about the new courthouse and the scandal involving Senator Thompson and his mismanagement of public funds?"

"Senator Thompson is a swine, all right. I don't know how you got that information from his staff, but it was brilliant. Nice piece of investigation, Katherine."

She beamed. "I was able to get it because the senator's staff also thinks he's a swine."

"But if he loses his next election, they'll certainly be out of a job."

"I know. They don't care."

The colonel shook his head with amazement. He slipped behind the printing press and took a quick swallow from his silver whiskey flask, then corked and hid it again.

"If you must drink, then do so in front of me, Father."

"All right," he said, getting his flask and openly taking another drink. "There!"

Katherine smiled tolerantly. "How is the pain today?"

"It'll disappear if I keep drinking."

"Only up to a certain point, and then your wonderful mind will also disappear."

The colonel had been about to say something, but changed his mind and smiled. "You know," he commented as he began to stack the papers, "I wish that I'd had you around these last few years."

"I wanted to be around, but you insisted that I go to that damned Eastern finishing school and then live with Grandma in Denver."

"I know. It was a mistake. I can see that now. But I want to tell you something, Katherine. No matter how hard you work, this paper is as doomed as I am with my cancer. I don't want you wasting your hopes and dreams on something that is bound to fail."

"Shut up!" Katherine's hand flew to her mouth. "I'm sorry," she said, rushing to throw her arms around her father's neck and hug him tightly. "I didn't mean that."

"Yes, you did, and I deserved it," the colonel whispered. "I'm sorry. Next time I start talking like that, throw a broom or something at me."

Katherine wiped tears from her eyes. "I'm going to sell the issues myself."

The colonel's pain-ravaged face reflected shock. When he protested, the tremor in his voice reflected his extreme weakness. "Katherine, you can't do that!"

"Why not?"

"Because . . . because you're my assistant editor! Editors don't hawk papers on the street corners. Katherine, that's a paperboy's job."

"We don't have any that are trustworthy. And besides," Katherine said, "we can't afford them. So for the time being at least, I'll be the paper-girl. And the printer and the reporter and your trustworthy assistant editor."

The colonel shook his head and his own eyes misted. "If you can hawk papers, then so can I."

"No," Katherine said firmly. "You need to save your strength."

"For what?" Chambers threw his long, slender arms into the air. "I'm going to die soon, so why not let me expend my life as I choose—hawking papers for a nickel a copy."

Katherine studied her father closely. He was quite weak, and she did not want him to have to walk about town and use his reserves unnecessarily. On the other hand, it was clear that he wanted to join her and show that he was not above selling his papers. That if his daughter had to do it, then so by God could he.

"All right," she said. "But there is a cold wind outside and I want you to bundle up. Coat, scarf around the neck, gloves to keep your hands warm."

"I'm not some frail old crone that will break under a cold breeze!" he proclaimed. "I'm a tough old bastard who is defying my cancer and who—with the courageous help of his dear but shortsighted daughter—will persevere and regain his name and literary reputation."

"Do as I say," Katherine said gently, as she reached for her own coat and pulled it on over her woolen sweater.

She had already decided to use an old wheelbarrow to transport papers as she sold them on the streets of Carson City. In the past, several paperboys had divided the load, but today she would have it all by herself.

Stepping out into the cold, stiff breeze, she began to load the wheelbarrow. "If we can just get people to buy this edition, they'll be eager to buy again."

"You are an optimistic angel," Chambers said, wincing to see his daughter's delicate hands grip the rough handles of the old wheelbarrow.

"Let's go!" Katherine urged, placing a smooth rock on the papers to keep them from blowing away.

They traveled up Carson Street past Washington, and stopped in front of the federal mint, where the presses faithfully converted the Comstock's diminishing silver output into shiny coinage.

"Hello there!" Katherine called to a group of businessmen. "Would you like to buy a paper?"

"Which paper?"

"*The Carson Courier.*"

"No thanks," one of the men said. "I hear enough of this town's gossip from my wife every night!"

Colonel Chambers bristled, and would have flown into a rage except that Katherine pushed in front of him and snatched a paper out of the wheelbarrow. With her prettiest smile, she held it up and said, "Look at the headlines! This isn't gossip, it's *news*! Don't you want to know about how taxpayers' money is being misspent? And about the dam that is being proposed just to the west of us on the Carson River? And what do you think about Senator Thompson's misuse of taxpayers' dollars?"

"Maybe I will take a copy," the man said, snatching the one from Katherine's hand.

"Me too," said the second man.

"Oh, why not?" the third man asked rhetorically. "If I don't buy one, these fellas will brand me a cheapskate."

"That's because you are!" the first man teased.

There was laughter, and other customers appeared. Katherine sold a half dozen papers in front of the federal mint, but that was just the beginning. As she pushed her wheelbarrow down the main street and called like a lifelong fish-peddler, Katherine's good looks and wide smile attracted customers in droves. By the time they were in front of the huge, silver-domed capitol building, half the newspapers were gone.

"I don't believe this," Colonel Chambers wheezed. "Your mother would turn over in her grave if she saw you pushing a wheelbarrow and peddling newspapers."

"No, she wouldn't. She'd be proud of the both of us for fighting to be competitive."

The colonel had to agree. In fact, as he recognized state senators and assemblymen coming from the capitol building, he began to intercept them and wave his paper in their faces.

"My daughter wrote most of this and it's brilliant! Just a nickel and you can find out what's *really* going on in Carson City!"

The papers sold. Pretty soon those who had bought them were talking about Senator Thompson, and others were actually coming to buy their own copies.

"It's working!" Katherine exclaimed happily. "And Father, I promise you that when our Wednesday issue appears, we're going to print and then sell *two hundred* copies."

"You're crazy!"

"No, dead serious," Katherine said, laughing and selling papers.

Everything was going better than they could have imagined until Senator Howard Thompson emerged from the capitol. He was a large man with a ruddy complexion, and was notorious for his quick and explosive temper. At the sight of the advancing politician, the colonel's smile died. Katherine followed her father's eyes and knew what was coming.

"I wrote this piece, so you just let me do the talking, Father. Everyone knows the man is a corrupt bully."

"Stay back, please!" Colonel Chambers ordered.

But Katherine had no intention of staying back while her father was berated or even physically attacked. She had seen this particular senator before, but had never exchanged words with him. To Katherine's way of thinking, Senator Thompson personified the public's conception of a greedy, self-serving, and immoral politician.

"What is this tripe?" Thompson roared, waving one of their papers that he must have gotten from an aide. "Goddammit, Colonel Chambers, I'll beat you to within an inch of your miserable, drunken life."

"No!" Katherine cried, throwing herself before her father. "You—"

Katherine didn't finish. The senator batted her roughly aside. She tripped and crashed over backward, striking her head on the cobblestone street.

"Katherine!"

Katherine was too stunned to rise. She felt dizzy when she attempted to reach back behind her head and feel how badly her scalp had been cut. She looked up to see her father being shaken like a rat in the grasp of the far larger and stronger Senator Thompson.

"Father!"

"You're going to Hell for writing this trash!" Thompson shouted, hurling the colonel aside. "I'll see you run out of town on a rail. I'll watch our inmates feed your diseased old body to the prison's hogs!"

Colonel Chambers struck the ground hard and skidded. When he looked up, one side of his face was covered with blood. He glared up at the senator and his waxen fingers reached inside his coat. Out came a pistol.

"No!" Thompson screamed, raising his hands as if he could shield himself from death.

But the colonel's bullet was already puncturing the senator's large stomach and then angling up along his spine. The colonel's second bullet was more to his liking, for it entered the senator's profane and open mouth, then blew a ragged hole out the back of his skull.

"There," the colonel said, placing the barrel of the revolver to his own head. "Now I guess Katherine will have another big story to write about on Wednesday."

And with that, he pulled the trigger and extinguished his own flickering spark of life.

# Chapter 13

Longarm and Bill waited for Jim Denton all the next morning. At noon, Berry said, "I think we ought to ride. If Denton can't get hisself here, we'll go and find him. If we can't, then we'll just go and wipe out the Quick gang by ourselves. We'll split the reward money two ways, instead of three. You game for that, Custis?"

"Sure, but do you know where they are?"

"I have a fair idea. They generally hide out in the mountains to the east. We're good enough trackers that we can cut their trail and find 'em. Lay an ambush and do what needs to be done."

"Maybe we should wait another day," Longarm suggested, hoping Jim Denton would still show up.

"Maybe," Berry said. "It would give me time to dip my wick at the Cat Corral."

Longarm blinked and belatedly realized that, if Berry went over there, all hell would break loose because the girls had been warned that he had murdered one of their own on the Comstock Lode.

"Uh . . . on second thought I think we'd better ride out now," Longarm said quickly. "I just have a feeling."

"You do?"

"Sure," Longarm said. "I've always operated on a sixth sense and it's telling me that we better not waste much time."

"Well," Berry said, casting a longing glance at the Cat Corral, "I don't see that it would take me more than a half hour to satisfy my needs. I could even catch up with you on down the trail."

"No," Longarm said insistently, "we have to ride *now*. And fast."

It was clear that Bill Berry was confused because of Longarm's sudden urgency, but he bowed to the pressure and said, "I guess maybe I can find something to poke out on the trail."

"Yeah," Longarm said with relief.

They rode out of Whiskeyville at a hard gallop, and continued southwest for the rest of the day. It was a dry, hard land with little water and a lot of empty land and sky. Now and then they came across a prospector and his burro, and twice they passed big ore wagons that were hauling ore samples to the stamping mills on the Comstock.

"How far to Wayout?" Berry called late that afternoon.

"About thirty miles!"

"Damn!" Berry swore. "I was hoping it was closer."

"Is that where you expect to meet up with Jim?"

"Yeah. He's sweet on a gal that's working in a saloon there. I'll bet that's why we ain't seen hide nor hair of him yet."

"Well," Longarm said, "if these horses don't quit on us, we ought to be in Wayout by early morning."

"We'd make camp if there was any damn water to be had in these parts," Berry said. "But there ain't, just the whiskey I got in my saddlebags. You want a pull?"

"Sure," Longarm said without enthusiasm.

For the next several hours they pulled on the whiskey and finished the entire bottle. Longarm made sure that Bill Berry got the lion's share of the liquor.

"I'll tell you something," Berry said, a loose grin on his face. "There's a certain freedom that comes with being your own law. Think about it."

"I have."

"So have I. As bounty hunters, all we got to do is worry about shootin' fast and straight. There ain't no judge or damn jury to face and answer a bunch of stupid questions. The only question a bounty hunter is asked is: Did you kill him or bring him in alive? That's it! Then you get a big reward. Everyone thanks you and says good riddance and you're on your way, lookin' for another sidewinder who needs his head chopped off. Neat, isn't it, Longarm?"

"Yeah, neat and clean."

"And there's another big advantage to being a bounty hunter that I bet you've never even thought about."

"What's that?"

"Well, there's the money that we pick off the bodies."

When Longarm just stared at him, Berry chuckled. "For example, do you know how much cash Jim and me made off One-Eared George and his friends?"

"No."

"They had robbed a lot of people and buried the money over by Eagle Peak. Of course, they didn't tell us that for a couple of days."

"You beat it out of them?" Longarm asked, recalling the severe beating of the dead outlaws mentioned by Billy Vail and others.

"Sure. Beat the hell outa 'em. In fact, it wasn't until we started to cut off George's ear that he got talkative."

"Is that right?"

"Yep. I had my bowie knife and he was all tied up tighter than a caterpillar in a cocoon. When my knife started to workin' its way down through his ear, George began to holler like crazy."

"Not surprising. Say, where is your bowie knife, Bill?"

The man's face stiffened. He blinked and looked hard at Longarm and said, "Damned if I didn't lose it a few days ago."

"Too bad," Longarm said. "But at least you got to use it on George's ear."

Berry relaxed. "You know, Custis, the really surprising thing was that I had it half cut off before he yelled, 'Eagle Peak! Our stash is at Eagle Peak!' "

Berry chuckled. "I left the ear on, but it was just flappin' around. Being as how he only had the one, George was pretty determined to keep that knife-sawed ear. I told him that it'd be better comin' off. Then Jim said that, if George was worried about what the ladies might think of his appearance, he should grow his hair longer so they wouldn't notice that both of his ears were missin'."

"I imagine he didn't take kindly to that suggestion."

"Naw. He really wanted at least one ear. So we bandaged his head and rode over to Eagle Peak."

"What did Heck say about all this?"

"Oh, he wasn't even there."

"He wasn't?"

"No," Berry said. "The old fool helped us catch old One-Eared and his friends, but then he took off. Said something about a girl."

Longarm took that to mean that Heck had gone to see the daughter he'd never known existed. "So just you and Jim Denton took the gang over to Eagle Peak?"

"That's right. George tried to escape a time or two, and so did the other two outlaws, but we caught 'em and made 'em pay for causin' us trouble."

"I see. And so you found a pile of their money buried at Eagle Peak?"

"Yep. George and his boys tried to go back on the deal, though. Refused to tell us exactly where it was buried. That's why I had to saw the rest of his ear off. I swear he was a stubborn man. But I'm surprise they didn't hear him hollering all the way to the Comstock Lode."

Berry laughed to himself while Longarm, who thought he'd heard about every kind of cruelty, had to struggle to keep a disarming smile on his face.

"Bill, how much money was buried at Eagle Peak?"

"There was one thousand two hundred thirty-six dollars, and a bag of pesos that George musta got off some Mexicans he killed. Custis, you should have seen Jim Denton and me when we got through counting up all that bounty! We just danced and whooped it up somethin' awful."

"And then you killed One-Eared—only he was No-Eared by then—along with his two friends."

"Yep. Wasn't anything else to do. If we'd have brought them in alive, they'd never have let us keep all the Eagle Peak money. They'd have tried to return it to whoever George and his boys stole it from."

"That's right."

"So we just killed George and his two friends and hauled 'em into Reno, where we sent the telegram to Billy Vail."

"I see."

"Haven't seen the three hundred dollars reward money from Billy yet, but it'll come. Billy is a pain in the ass sometimes, but he's an honest man."

"That he is," Longarm agreed.

They rode on a few minutes in silence and then Berry said, "I wonder how much stagecoach money this Wade Quick fella and his brothers have hidden out in the hills?"

"Maybe they've already spent it."

"If they have, it'll go even harder on 'em." Berry growled. "There's a lot worse ways to die than a quick bullet in the brain."

"That there is," Longarm agreed.

"I just hope, for this Quick fella's sake, that he's got some money squirreled."

"Me too," Longarm said, shaking his head.

That night, Berry cracked another bottle, and fell off his horse and went to sleep a few hours before daybreak. Longarm didn't care because he was also worn out. So he hobbled, then unsaddled, their hungry and thirsty horses. Afterward, he laid his head on his saddle and fell soundly asleep, and did not awaken until mid-morning.

"Come on, Bill," he said, nudging the man with his toe. "We got to get these horses some feed and water. They're starting to suffer."

Berry groaned. "*I'm* suffering. Too damn much whiskey."

"Yep," Longarm said without the least bit of sympathy. "Too damn much."

Wayout was little more than a dusty street lined by about a dozen sagging tents. At the edge of town there was an old man in bib overalls sitting on a wagon of loose hay and hawking it by the armful. For another four bits, he'd sell your horse all the water it could drink along with a bucket of grain.

"Let's take care of the horses before ourselves," Longarm said as Berry began to rein toward the tent saloons.

"Here," Berry replied, dismounting and handing Longarm a twenty-dollar gold piece. "You take care of the horses and keep the change."

"You're a real generous man."

"That's what the ladies think," Berry joked painfully. "And since I quit the feds, I can afford to be generous. I'll see if I can scout up Jim."

Longarm watched Berry saunter off toward the saloons, and then he went over to the man selling horse feed. "How's business, old-timer?"

"Getting better about now, I expect."

The old man had a full, white beard and bright blue eyes. There was a corncob pipe jammed between his teeth and a slouch hat pulled low over his brow.

"Looks like good hay," Longarm said.

"It is good hay," the old man replied. "If'n it weren't, you might shoot me."

"Maybe."

"Instead, you'll pay my price because you and your partner both have good-looking horses and I expect that you need them to make your livin'."

"Why do you say that?"

"I can tell that neither one of you are prospectors, that's for sure. You look like gunfighters to me."

"We're not. Do you happen to know where we can find Wade Quick and his brothers?"

The old man chuckled. "You think I'd be stupid enough to tell you? Why, if'n I did and you didn't kill 'em, they'd come and kill *me*."

"Just answer me this," Longarm said. "Is the Quick gang here in Wayout?"

"Nope."

"Are they in these parts?"

"How much money you carryin'?"

Longarm sighed and dug into his pockets. He brought out the twenty-dollar gold piece that he'd just been given and held it up to glitter in the bright midday sunlight.

"I want information and enough feed and water for these horses until tomorrow."

"All right," the old man said. "The Quick boys aren't in town yet and I don't expect that they will be for a couple of weeks."

"Why?"

"They rode out only three days ago."

"How many are riding in the gang?"

"There's Wade and his brothers Herman and Melvin. Usually, they got another three or four gunnies or more with 'em for extra protection."

"All good fighters?"

"Damn good. Wade is as fast with a gun as any man I've ever seen, and I've seen more than a few."

"Describe him."

"He looks like you, 'cept he isn't as big. Wears a pearl-handled pistol on his right hip. Most always wears a red or purple bandanna around his neck and there are silver conchos in his hatband."

Longarm was satisfied with the description. It sounded as if Wade Quick would be a man who stood out in a crowd.

"Now let me ask you something," the old man said.

"Askin' is free."

"Are you and that fella that you rode in with going to try and take on the whole durned gang?"

"We might have some help."

"You better have one hell of a lot of help!"

Longarm watched the horses drink. He had to pull them back after about ten gulps because he didn't want them to take in too much water too fast. It could colic an animal, and besides, they also needed some feed.

"Don't you worry about these horses," the old man said, reading Longarm's concern as he took a handful of reins. "I'll take care of 'em proper. Won't let them eat nor drink too much all at one time."

"Thanks," Longarm said, taking his fine Winchester from its saddle boot.

"That's about the prettiest Model '73 I ever laid eyes upon," the old man said with admiration.

"It is a beauty. I haven't even had a chance to shoot the thing yet."

"Better try 'er out before you come across the Quick gang or you may be sorry."

"You've got a point," Longarm conceded. He levered a shell, threw the rifle to his shoulder, and fired in one smooth motion.

Seventy yards away, a discarded tin can skipped high in the air and before it landed, the Winchester roared a second time and the can acted like it had been jerked sideways on an invisible wire.

"Damn!" the old man whispered. "You sure are something with that rifle."

Longarm grinned. "You should see me with a Colt."

"I'd be pleasured!"

"Another time," Longarm said as men poked their heads out of the tents to stare.

"Sure," the old man said with a grin.

Longarm levered another shell into the chamber, and headed for the tent where he'd last seen Bill Berry disappear.

# Chapter 14

"Why, as I live and breath, if it isn't Deputy Marshal Custis Long, the pride of federal law enforcement," Jim Denton exclaimed with a trace of sarcasm in his voice when he saw Longarm. "So what brings you to this neck of the woods, Deputy Marshal?"

"Like I told Bill, I've been working on a case," Longarm said, not bothering to extend his hand to the short, barrel-chested man he'd once fought beside. Jim Denton was quick and smart, a whole lot smarter than Bill Berry, and Longarm knew that he would have to be very careful.

Denton wiped beer foam from his walrus-brown mustache. "You told our friend that you're in Nevada on a case. Exactly who are you after?"

"Just a small-time train robber."

"Bill says his name is Homer Perkins."

"That's right."

Denton scratched his jaw and frowned. "Never even heard of the man."

"He was robbing trains up in Wyoming. We lost track of him for about six months and then got a tip that he was living in Nevada. You know how they move around."

"Sure I do. It's our business to know. Has this Perkins fella got a reward on his head?"

"A couple hundred dollars."

"That's enough." Denton shrugged. "Maybe, after we settle up with the Quick gang, we'll go help you find him."

"That's small money cut three ways."

"Yeah, the reward is small money," Denton agreed, "but that's only part of the payoff. Custis, I know Bill told you about all the money we took off One-Eared George and his two compadres."

"He did. Even split two ways, that's more than you made in an entire year as a law officer."

"Yep." Denton sipped his beer thoughtfully and regarded Longarm with a calm, steady eye. "I hear you were surprised when Bill told you that we'd handed in our badges."

"That's true."

"It's kind of surprising that no one in Denver happened to mention our resignations, don't you think?"

Longarm's voice hardened because Denton wasn't asking friendly or curious questions, he was interrogating. "If you've got an itch, scratch the damn thing, Jim."

Denton raised his eyebrows and smiled. "It's no itch. It's just that something about your story is rubbing me a little the wrong way. I can't quite understand why you wouldn't have heard about us resigning our offices by now."

"Like I told Bill, I've been riding some long lonesome trails off in the backwaters for a while. Mostly in places where you'll find no telegraphs, no trains, no newspapers. Nothing but bad liquor and worse women. Now, if you're trying to put a burr under my saddle, Jim, you're doing a real good job of it and I'll damn sure—"

"Easy, Custis!" Denton said, forcing a smile. "Don't you get your dander up. Bill and I both agree that you're going to be a great help with this Quick gang. Thing of it is, they're real hard cases. They shoot and ask questions later. But capturing them is worth the risk because I figure that, in the last six months, they've taken about five thousand dollars from the stage lines."

"That's a lot of cash."

"You bet it is," Denton said. "And we're hoping that they ain't spent every last cent of it already. Could be that we're looking at a real payday."

"That would suit me just fine."

"Good!" Denton smiled. "I just never figured that you'd quit the feds, Custis. You being their number-one man and such a good and loyal friend of Billy Vail. Know what I mean?"

"I'm not sure. What are you driving at, Jim?"

"Just that I wouldn't want any misunderstanding to come between us. I mean, we're all old brothers of the badge. And we just want to make damn sure that we don't have to spill each other's blood. Right?"

Longarm managed to nod his head. It was obvious that Jim Denton, unlike Bill Berry, did not trust him. Denton was making it crystal clear that he didn't believe his story about chasing a supposed train robber from Wyoming down into Nevada. And he'd also made it very clear that he would have no hesitation about shooting Longarm down if he stepped out of line.

"I guess you heard about your old partner, Heck Wilcox?"

"I heard that he worked with you to capture One-Eared and then he left to do a job on his own. I also heard something about a girl."

"That randy old rooster found out that he'd fathered a child! Heck has probably sired a passel of kids, but the mother of this one came back and gave him some damn story about how this kid was real sick and needed some money."

"I see. Where is Heck now?"

"He's off somewhere hunting another bounty. The independent bastard decided to go off on his own. Said his bounty wasn't big enough to split three ways. He wouldn't talk to us, so we sure didn't feel obligated to give Heck a share of what we found at Eagle Peak. And we'd appreciate it if you didn't say anything to him when we meet up."

"You expecting to cross trails soon?"

Denton ignored Longarm's question. "I think there has been enough talking. The truth is, I wish to hell Bill here would learn to keep his big mouth shut."

Bill Berry colored, and it was clear to Longarm that Denton had climbed all over his partner for flapping his gums and making loose whiskey talk. Clearly, it would have made sense if Berry hadn't said a thing to anyone about all the money they'd gotten from One-Eared before they'd killed him and his two outlaw partners.

"Don't worry," Longarm said, "I wouldn't even want to be around if Heck found out that you and Bill split over a thousand dollars he didn't know about."

"Good," Denton said, obviously relieved. "Now, are you ready to make some *real* money?"
"I am."
"Then let's see that badge of yours."
"What?"
Denton stuck out his hand. "Let's see it."
Longarm figured he had no choice but to go along with whatever Jim Denton had in mind. If he refused to give up his badge the game was up, and Longarm wasn't yet ready to lay his cards on the table and call for a showdown.
"Here you go."
Denton took Longarm's badge and inspected it. "The silver finish is rubbing off."
"It's had hard use and a lot of polishing."
"It's tarnished and needs to finally be put to rest," Denton said as he dropped Longarm's badge into a spittoon.
Denton watched as the badge sank in the vile mixture. When he looked up at Longarm, he was smiling. "Well, Custis, now you're an ex-deputy marshal with all the privileges of the ordinary citizen, including the right to earn a federal, state, or local bounty by whatever means necessary."
"I guess I am," Longarm managed to say even as he remembered that it had been Heck Wilcox himself who had once proudly pinned that badge on his chest.
"Where's that girl that you're so sweet on?" Bill asked, wanting to brighten up the conversation.
"She's getting a couple of her friends and tonight she's promised that we're going to have us a little party. Bill, I knew you'd appreciate that before we ride out after the Quick gang tomorrow morning."

Berry grinned and said to Longarm, "I knew we'd find something to poke out here."

"Yeah," Longarm said without enthusiasm. "And I can just imagine what the available women in Wayout look like."

Denton laughed. "They ain't much, that's for sure. But in the dark, who cares?"

"Yeah," Berry said, licking his lips with anticipation.

Longarm wanted to get back to the subject of Heck Wilcox. "Tell me this, Jim. Why don't we try and find Heck now instead of waiting until we just happen to meet up with him? It sounds like we can use all the help we can get if we're going to take on the Quick gang."

"Might be a good idea," Denton said noncommittally. "It all kind of depends."

"On what?"

"On the way things go this next week," Denton said evasively. "But I'll give the matter some serious thought."

Longarm knew that he'd pushed Jim Denton as hard and as far as he'd dared. To do any more would likely be inviting a bullet in the back. So for now, he guessed he'd just have to wait and play this game out according to Denton's schedule. However, if things went well, he'd not only be in a position to capture a very ruthless gang, but also to arrest Bill Berry for the murder of Liz Alcott and to meet Heck face to face.

The risk was great, but so was the potential payoff.

That night, they had a belly-slapping tent party. It wasn't what Longarm wanted, and the three women were unwashed, rough, and smelly. Longarm had it in his mind to tell his woman that he was not feeling well, but she didn't give him a chance to make an excuse. Instead, she damned near raped him. He could hear Jim Denton and Bill Berry riding their women for all they were worth. Listening to their grunts and panting excited Longarm enough to do his manly duty.

"You're a slow starter, but you warm up fast," the woman grunted as Longarm rolled her over and began to hump her with a good deal more passion than he'd expected to generate.

"It's been a long ride," he said, wondering how many weeks it had been since she'd taken a bath. "And to be honest, I'm all played out."

The woman under him laughed and grabbed his muscular buttocks. "Honey, you don't know what 'played out' even means. By morning, I'll have your tongue hangin' down to your knees and your big root as limp and withered as a year-old carrot."

Longarm had to smile. He heard Jim Denton roar with pleasure and then his woman cry out either in pain or ecstasy, it was impossible to tell which.

"Come on, honey, don't listen to our friends havin' all the fun. Today is gone and tomorrow might never come around. So do me hard!"

Longarm realized that the woman was right. With a growl that formed deep down in his chest, he began to slam his big rod in and out of the woman until she cried out in pleasure as he filled her with his seed.

# Chapter 15

Longarm knew they were three sorry-looking amigos when they finally left the little mining town of Wayout. He was very sore and bleary-eyed from one of the hardest nights of lovemaking he'd ever known.

"Whew," Berry said, "I'm about shanked down to a nubbin. How about you fellas?"

"I feel like my pole has been pounded into sawdust," Jim Denton said. "How you feelin', Custis?"

"I'm feelin' low and slow."

They all laughed, knowing they looked like hell and that their wild night of pleasure was worth the pain. For the rest of that day things were easy between them, and Longarm could almost believe that they were still federal deputy marshals setting out to catch a band of murdering stagecoach robbers. But then, out of the blue would come the realization that Bill Berry was a woman-killer, and that Jim Denton had somehow turned a corner and would stop at nothing to collect a bounty no matter how much blood was shed.

That night they slept in the hills like dead men. The next morning Longarm awoke first and made a breakfast of fried beans, bread, and strong black coffee.

"Wake up, ladies," he ordered. "We can't afford to sleep the whole damn day away."

Denton was the first to stir, and when he opened his eyes and saw his breakfast plate, he said, "Custis, you always were one to get up before everyone else. You know who I dreamed about last night?"

"Nope."

"That rich and pretty New Mexico rancher's daughter that was so sweet on you a couple of years ago."

"What brought her to mind?"

"I dunno. Tell me, Custis, why is it that you never married that girl? She couldn't get enough of you, but you rode off and left her."

"Aggie was a little crazy."

"She was?"

"Yep. The girl was a looker all right, and her father would have made me ranch foreman, but Aggie had some pretty strange desires."

"For example?" Berry asked, reaching for his cup of coffee.

Longarm frowned. "Remember her father?"

"Why, sure."

"Remember that huge dog of his?"

Denton frowned. "Yeah. Part wolf, wasn't he?"

"That's right. Well, one night I discovered that Aggie had a special fondness for that dog."

Denton thought a moment, and then he said, "Well I'll be damned! Little Miss Fancy Pants was doin' it with her father's dog?"

"I didn't say that."

"But that's what you were suggesting."

Longarm sipped his coffee and studied the sky. "There are storm clouds moving at us from the east. Could be we'll have some rain this afternoon. Do either of you boys have any idea how much farther we'll have to ride in order to flush the Quick gang?"

"We'll be at their hideout before noon," Denton said, still obviously astounded by what he'd heard about the New Mexico rancher's daughter.

"You want to tell me what to expect before we get there, or is it supposed to be a big surprise?"

"Not much to say," Denton replied. "Believe it or not, the Quick family used to run cattle in this dry sagebrush land. They homesteaded on Rock Creek. There's enough grass and water to run a couple hundred head of cows or horses."

"Why didn't the brothers stick to ranching?" Longarm asked.

"The Paiutes kept raiding their spread," Denton answered. "Indians killed both their parents about ten years ago and tortured their sisters to death before they drove off the last of their livestock."

"So they turned to robbing stages," Longarm said.

Denton nodded. "They're a lot better at it than they ever were at ranching. Mostly they operate up around Austin and Eureka. There are lots of little stage lines in that country and plenty of prospectors totin' around gold nuggets."

"But now and then," Berry interrupted, "Wade takes the whole gang and rides over to Reno, Carson City, or up to the Comstock Lode for a big payday."

"That's right," Denton said. "And that's why the state and the county have put up rewards on the gang."

"It sounds like easy money," Longarm said.

"Not that easy," Denton replied. "These boys are marksmen, and they damn sure won't surrender to the three of us without putting up a hard fight."

"Any ideas how to take them?" Longarm asked.

"I think we ought to stake their spread out and watch them today, then probably hit them first thing tomorrow morning while they're still asleep."

"What about guards?"

"I doubt they'll post any."

"And dogs?" Experience had given Longarm a healthy respect for watchdogs.

"We'll have to find out about 'em when we get there," Denton said. "I'd expect them to have a few. Wade Quick is reckless, but he's not stupid."

Longarm nodded with understanding. He finished his breakfast and coffee, then scoured his plate with sand and went to saddle his horse.

"Ain't no hurry," Berry yelled. "Jim says that the Quick ranch is only about three hours ride from here."

"I'd still like to get going," Longarm said. "If there's a bunch of them, we're going to need a far better plan than just rushing in at daybreak with our six-guns blazing. And there's always the chance that they'll be off robbing a stagecoach someplace."

"If they are, all the better," Denton said. "That would mean they'd have more money for us."

"Yeah!" Berry said with illumination. "I guess it would!"

Denton looked over at Longarm and rolled his eyes. Bill Berry was a handsome man and the ladies liked him, but he had never been known for his intelligence.

"Let's ride," Longarm said, casting the dregs of the coffeepot into the brush and loading their supplies.

"Custis," Denton said, "what you don't seem to understand is that I'm givin' the orders from now on. It's either that, or you're out."

"How come?"

"This is our party, and you just happened to come along and share the prize. When you set up your own party, *you* can call the shots."

"All right," Longarm snapped, acting as if he were angry. "But I want to know what to expect."

"If the Quick boys and their outlaw friends are at the ranch, you had damn sure better expect a shootout," Denton said. "There will be no asking them to surrender. They don't know the meaning of the word."

"I sure wish that Heck Wilcox was with us," Berry said. "That old heller had no equal in a gun battle."

"That's for sure," Longarm said.

"Well, he ain't with us, so the both of you can quit whinin' about it," Denton snapped.

Berry's cheeks reddened with anger and he shot a sideways glance at Longarm, who ignored him because he had his own troubles. It went against his grain as a lawman to simply charge into the Quick gang at daybreak and open fire, slaughtering as many as he could before they could rally. It went real hard against the grain. And yet, Denton had made it very clear that this was their only chance for victory.

Longarm chewed on that worrisome bone, until he decided that he would just have to play the cards as they were dealt to him. If there weren't many of the gang at the ranch, he'd make sure that they weren't all gunned down. But if there were a large number of outlaws, then Denton's plan was the only one that made sense. Three men, even if they were ex-federal deputy marshals, weren't going to intimidate a bunch of killers, robbers, and rapists.

"The Quick ranch is just over that low rise of hills," Denton said about noontime. "We'd better tie the horses to these pinyon trees and go the rest of the way on foot."

"Fine with me," Longarm muttered.

"You still mad about me being in charge?" Denton challenged.

"Just make the right decisions," Longarm snapped.

"And if I don't?"

"Then you'll damn sure have a lot more than the Quick brothers to worry about."

Denton's eyes shuttered. "You always were bull-headed and wanting to run the damn show."

"Like Heck Wilcox, I can back my promises."

"Yeah, well, in case you forgot, Heck got some pretty good deputy marshals killed in the line of duty out of his stubbornness and impatience."

"And he saved one hell of a lot of them, including me."

"Just follow my orders," Denton said as they tied their horses. "I know I can depend on Bill, but you worry me."

"Jim, quit jawin' and lead off," Longarm ordered as he finished tying his horse.

Denton led the way up the side of the rocky, brush-choked hillside. When they neared the top, he went to his knees and removed his sweat-stained hat and crawled on up to the crown. A few minutes later, Longarm and Berry joined him.

Longarm was surprised at how pretty the Quick homestead was given the hard surrounding country. A spring fed a creek that ran through a grassy valley that was about a mile long and a quarter mile wide. There were a few dozen cattle grazing along the creek, and the Quick family had built a sturdy log cabin. It was small, maybe two rooms, but it looked to be well made and it had a rock fireplace.

"I count an even dozen horses in the corrals," Berry said. "It looks to me as if the whole gang is holed up there right now."

"Yeah," Denton said. "And I'd say that some of them got shot up from their last raid. Maybe that whittled the odds down in our favor a mite."

"There's still a bunch," Berry said as they watched several of the men digging three graves for dead gang members.

"It's hard to say how many might be inside, but I count eight in the yard," Longarm said. "I take it that fella with the red bandanna is Wade Quick."

"Yep," Denton said, "and he's a dead shot. I've seen him throw a coin into the sky and drill it dead center."

"Shooting a coin is one thing. Shooting a man who is shooting back at you is another."

Denton snorted. "Let me tell you something, Custis. Wade Quick and his brothers have been shot at plenty and they've always come out on top."

"Wonder how much money they got on this job?" Berry asked. "I sure hope it was a pile."

Longarm picked out two other men who bore at least a faint resemblance to Wade Quick. He pointed them out to his companions and said, "Are those Wade's brothers?"

"Yep," Berry said. "Don't be fooled by how young they look. They're deadly as baby rattlers."

"I'll keep that in mind." Longarm's brow furrowed. "I see two ranch dogs. Big ones."

"That means we'll just have to do the best we can not to alert the gang until we're across that yard and jumping through their cabin door," Denton said. "We'll also have to dig up those three bodies."

"Why?" Longarm asked.

"Because we can get a hundred dollars reward apiece for them."

"But they'll be filthy with dirt," Berry protested. "Jim, it'll be obvious that they'd already been planted."

"Look," Denton said, "we'll just toss 'em in Rock Creek and roll 'em around a little, then strap 'em over a horse. They'll dry clean enough. We're damn sure not leaving three hundred dollars to rot in those graves."

Longarm couldn't believe the conversation. He inched back from the crown of the hill, then came to his feet and returned to their horses. He unsaddled his sorrel and pitched his saddle down for a pillow. Spreading his horse blankets on the rocky ground, he stretched out for a long nap.

"Well, ain't he the cool one!" Berry crowed. "Ain't you even worried about someone comin' round and seeing us?"

"Nope." Longarm placed his hat down over his face. "I'm more worried that you brought along whiskey and will get drunk and become worthless before we jump into this fight."

"Dammit!" Berry swore. "I got whiskey but I'm not going to have a drop until we've wiped out that gang."

"Me neither," Denton said. "We're all going to stay sober. There's too much money on the line here to mess it up. And besides, these boys are tough."

"Good," Longarm said with a yawn. "Now leave me in peace so I can take a long nap."

"Sure," Denton said. "A man needs his beauty sleep."

"I always said that old Custis was just as cool as a cucumber in a root cellar," Bill Berry said as he walked away.

Longarm closed his eyes and prepared to nap. He didn't trust either of these men, but he knew they'd need his gun tomorrow morning when they attacked the Quick cabin. They'd need his gun and a whole lot of luck.

# Chapter 16

When Longarm awoke the next morning, he felt totally refreshed. The stars were dying and there was a faint streak of pale pink edging along the eastern horizon. He sat up realizing that it would be fully light in less than an hour.

"Hey! Wake up!"

"Huh?" Denton muttered groggily.

Longarm climbed to his feet and went over to his two sleeping companions. Jim Denton was sitting, but Bill Berry was trying to roll over and go back to sleep.

"Come on, Bill!" Longarm snapped. "If we don't get movin', we'll lose our chance for surprise and have to wait another entire day."

The two ex-deputy marshals managed to rouse themselves into wakefulness. When Denton saw the light in the eastern sky, he snapped into action. "All right," he said, "let's go! Custis, you bringing that shotgun?"

"Yeah."

"Nothing like a scattergun in close quarters. You ready, Bill?"

"No."

"Too damn bad," Denton snapped. "Let's go!"

Berry was half asleep, but they were running out of time. Maybe the ranch dogs wouldn't see them, but the chances were that they would and they'd wake the place up with their barking.

"When we top the ridge, we just start running as fast and as quiet as we can," Denton said. "With luck, the dogs won't hear or see us and we'll get to the ranch house before they set up a ruckus."

"That's it?" Longarm asked. "That's the plan?"

"You got any better ideas?"

"Yeah, we should have charged down the hill on our horses. We could have gotten to the cabin a lot faster."

"But the dogs would have heard the hoofbeats as soon as we topped that hill."

Longarm had to admit that Denton might have a point. Everything depended on the dogs. If they were alert, there would be no element of surprise. If, however, the dogs were lazy and inattentive, Longarm was thinking that they had an excellent chance of going all the way and making short work of the ruthless outlaw gang.

As they ran silently down the hill and onto the grassy valley floor, Longarm could have surged out into the lead, but he chose to pace himself and stay abreast of Denton and Berry. They crossed the open grass separating the sage from the ranch cabin.

It was not until they hit the yard with their breath raggedly tearing in and out of their lungs that the dogs came out from under the front porch, growling as they attacked.

Longarm didn't want to squander one of his

precious shotgun shells on the dogs so he let Berry and Denton open fire and drop them. Longarm surged ahead, landed on the porch, and kicked the front door half off its hinges.

"United States marshals, everyone freeze!" he shouted, jumping through the doorway and throwing himself sideways as a volley of gunfire stabbed through the darkness.

When Longarm hit the floor, he opened fire with the double-barreled shotgun. A huge double stab of flame swept across the cramped interior of the cabin and leveled everything in its path.

Outlaws. Furniture. Everything.

The outlaws screamed even louder when Denton and Berry charged through the doorway with their six-guns blazing. Longarm heard the sound of glass shattering. He heard the pounding of running feet and before he dared to stand, the drum of galloping hooves.

"Some of them are getting away!" Denton shouted into their semi-darkness. "Bill, get after them!"

A table skidded along on the floor as Berry slammed blindly into it. "Sonofabitch!" he grunted.

Yellow flames of gunfire kept leaping out of the darkness, and Longarm felt a bullet whip-crack past his ear. He ducked and drew his six-gun, firing rapidly. He didn't know how many of the gang were still alive, but there had to be at least three or four.

"Bill, get after them!" Denton shouted as another man tried to escape but was brought down by gunfire before he could leap through the shattered window.

Berry cursed and lunged for the door. For an

instant, he was skylighted in the rectangular wedge of the door, his silhouette framed against the pale morning sky. Guns opened up from across the room, and Longarm saw Berry throw his hands up to grab both sides of the door frame. More bullets shrieked across the room and Berry danced on his toes, then pitched headlong onto the porch, dead before he landed.

"You sonofabitches!" Denton screamed, emptying his six-gun and then finding a second weapon.

For the next minute, there was a furious exchange of gunfire across the room. It was close, deadly work. The firefight might have lasted indefinitely had not Longarm been holding a double-barreled shotgun. There was less return gunfire each time he emptied the devastating close-quarters weapon.

Finally, a man cried, "I surrender! No more! Please!"

"Stand up!" Denton yelled at the silhouetted figure across the room. "All of you, stand up!"

"I'm the only one left," the man sobbed. "Please don't kill me!"

"What's your name?"

"Don. Don Arnold!"

Longarm started to order the man to step forward with his hands in the air, but Jim Denton's chuckle sent a shiver down his spine.

"Well, Mr. Arnold, kiss your bloody ass good-bye."

"No!" Longarm shouted.

It was too late. Denton pumped two slugs into the man and drove him back to the wall, where he slid down to a sitting position.

"Dammit, Jim! We could have used him for information! Some of them got away!"

"They're heading back to Wayout," Denton said, quickly reloading both his guns. "That's the only place left for them to run."

Longarm came to his feet. It was so dim in the cabin that it took him a few minutes to find all the dead outlaws and then to drag them out into the ranch yard.

"Sonofabitch," Denton said. "Wade got away and so did one of his brothers."

"Are you sure that they'll go to Wayout?"

"Yeah. They've got friends there who will hide 'em. Let's dig up the three they buried yesterday and load the whole bunch in a wagon."

"I'm not digging up any corpses no matter what the reward. What about Bill?"

Denton's answer shocked even Longarm. "We can pass his body off as being a gang member and get paid an extra hundred dollars. So let's forget about the three that's buried and get after Wade and his kid brother."

Longarm ground his teeth. He stared at the bullet-riddled bodies, and his eyes came to rest on the man who had tried to surrender inside the cabin. An inner rage filled Longarm. He walked up to Denton and backhanded the man so hard he split Denton's lips and sent him staggering backward. When Denton recovered enough to reach for his six-gun, he found himself staring at the muzzle of Longarm's Colt.

"We're finished," Denton choked. "We're going to take these bodies all the way to Carson City and collect the reward, then call it quits."

"Suits me down to the ground," Longarm said. "But we're not going anywhere until we bury Bill."

"*You* bury him! I'll hitch up the team and load the bodies."

Longarm holstered his gun. He was sure that it wouldn't take long to find a shovel and dig a shallow grave. Maybe it could be argued that Bill Berry didn't deserve to be buried because he'd stabbed Liz Alcott to death. But the man had been a good deputy United States marshal for many years, and Longarm felt that Berry was at least owed an unmarked grave.

Denton loaded the six outlaws into the wagon while Longarm roped together all the saddle horses on a single lead line.

Denton's mouth was a bloody pulp and when he spoke, it caused his mashed lips bleed faster. "When we get to Wayout, I'm killin' Wade myself. I'll brook no interference."

"I don't give a damn what you will or will not brook," Longarm replied. "If we can take Wade and his kid brother alive, we'll do it. If not, we'll gun them down together."

Denton's eyes blazed with hatred, and Longarm saw something in them that said that he, and not the Quick brothers, was Jim Denton's next target.

# Chapter 17

Longarm dug a deep and proper grave for Bill Berry and lowered him down easy. There wasn't time to build the ex-lawman a simple cross or grave marker, but at least he could say a few words of prayer in behalf of a man that had once been his friend and fellow deputy marshal.

"Lord," he whispered, closing his eyes and bowing his head, "I guess I should have asked Bill why he stabbed that poor Virginia City saloon girl. You'll be the judge as to what happens to Bill's soul—if he ever had one."

Longarm struggled to think of something good to say in the late Bill Berry's behalf. Finally, he said, "Lord, Bill was an honest and upright deputy United States marshal for a lot of years before he went bad. He shot some outlaws that I'm sure would have done in some righteous Christians. I hope you'll take that into consideration."

Longarm opened his eyes and reached for the shovel. He punched it into the fresh pile of dirt and tossed a shovelful onto Berry's chest. He started to pitch a second shovelful when he heard the sound of a gun cocking.

"Turn around," Jim Denton softly ordered.

Longarm turned and saw the Denton had caught him off guard and with nothing better than an old shovel in his hands. "Jim, it looks to me as if you're planning to claim my body as one of the Quick gang for another hundred dollars."

Denton barked a cruel laugh. "Not a chance. You're too damn well known, Custis. But as I was hitching the wagon to take all the bodies back, I kept noticing what a fine job you were doing on that grave."

"Glad you think so."

"Oh, I do! I'm so lazy that I'd only have dug one about a yard deep. Just enough to cover up poor Bill. But you must have dug Bill's grave a good five feet deep. You even squared the corners. Custis, you always were one to do things the right rather than the easy way."

"The right way usually *is* the easy way, at least in the long run."

Denton raised his eyebrows and chuckled. He was having fun. "I don't agree with that, but I have always believed in letting a man hold to his own opinions."

"Bullshit," Longarm said without rancor. "You're the kind of fella who either wins an argument with words or resorts to force. There was always just Jim Denton's way, or no way at all."

Denton laughed, but the gun trained on Longarm remained very steady. "You might just have a point there! Fact is, I gave our working arrangement some serious thought in the last half hour while I was hitching up the team."

"I can see that. But I don't like the conclusion that

you seemed to have reached."

"Actually, I don't either. Killing you brings me no joy, Custis. I wish we could work together as bounty hunters. We'd be unstoppable. You're twice the man that Bill Berry was. But you're too damned independent."

"Sort of like Heck Wilcox?"

"Exactly!" Denton exclaimed, looking pleased by the comparison. "He and I just naturally collided over most every issue. And we decided to just part company before we killed each other."

"But you're not going to let me go, are you?" Longarm wasn't asking a question. He was trying to buy a little time, though he did not know for what purpose because he was already as good as dead.

"No," Denton answered, "I just can't. You'd betray me. You'd have to be honest with the state officials in Carson City. That would cost me a bundle of reward money. Who knows, it might also cost me my life."

Denton waited for Longarm to deny the charge. When he did not, Denton said, "I used to admire you and Heck Wilcox. I thought you were the toughest, most honorable men I'd ever known. But that opinion changed a few years ago."

"Why?"

"I looked at Heck and realized that he'd become just another broke old man. That after risking his life to uphold the law for all those years, he still didn't have a pot to piss in. Why, he couldn't even help this daughter that suddenly showed up."

"Maybe you and Bill should have helped him out."

"He wouldn't have accepted our help. There was no point in even offering. The old fool is just too damn proud."

"So where did he go?"

"After an outlaw named Garn Tilford who shot up a little mining town named Quartzite and robbed the bank. Tilford gunned down four people including a woman who just happened to be making a deposit. The woman's father has big mining money. He's offered a five-hundred-dollar reward for Tilford's head, no questions asked."

"I see."

"Not quite," Denton said with a faint grin. "What I haven't told you yet is that, after I go and shoot down Wade Quick and his brother, then take the whole pile of their stinkin' bodies to Carson City for the reward money, I'm going to find Heck."

"And kill him," Longarm said, suddenly realizing what Denton really had in mind.

"Yes. But I won't make my move until after Heck tracks down and kills Garn Tilford."

"What if he has already, and has collected the five hundred dollars in reward money and spent it? Or sent it to his daughter?"

Denton turned philosophical. "Hell, Custis, you know as well as I do that no man can win 'em all. I'll still have a lot of reward money in my pockets in addition to that Eagle Peak cash that Bill and I never quite got around to spending. Custis, with all that, I'll be a pretty wealthy ex-lawman."

"Yeah, I guess you will at that," Longarm said, tightening his grip on the shovel.

Denton cocked the hammer of his pistol. "Do you want to stretch out in that grave with Bill and make this easy for us both?"

"The grave is already occupied."

"Yeah, but you'll both fit."

Longarm knew that he was out of time. "Listen," he said in a voice that he hoped sounded like a frightened plea. "Please don't—"

"Don't beg," Denton said. "You've lived well, try to die well."

Longarm whipped both his shovel and its dirt right at Denton's face even as the man's pistol bucked. Longarm heard Denton's shout of pain as the shovel struck him, but at the same instant he felt a bullet strike him in the left shoulder and spin him completely around. Losing his balance, Longarm toppled into the grave, landing on Bill Berry as Denton fired a second time but missed.

Dragging his own six-gun up, Longarm struggled with revulsion as he crawled across Berry's stiffening corpse. Longarm's natural impulse was to jump up, but that would have been fatal. Instead, Longarm waited an instant, then stuck his head up just high enough to look out of the grave and fired at Denton as rapidly as he could pull the trigger.

Denton was madly trying to scrape his eyes free of dirt. He was cursing and firing blind. Longarm's bullets punched into his chest three times stitching a neat little pattern. Denton dropped to his knees, emptied his gun into the ranch yard, and then toppled forward.

Longarm couldn't scramble out of Bill Berry's grave fast enough. He grabbed his wounded shoulder, tearing away his jacket to reveal that a slug had passed through a lot of muscle but no bone. The wound was bleeding heavily, but Longarm quickly stanched the flow of blood with his bandanna.

Longarm went to the stream that fed this isolated, high desert valley. He washed away blood and the dirt of Berry's grave, then walked slowly back to the wagon. For several moments, he stood alone among a bunch of dead bodies trying to decide what was the best thing to do all the way around. He damn sure wasn't interested in transporting a pile of corpses all the way to Carson City. And there was still Berry's corpse to cover, and the matter of Jim Denton.

"If I deliver these fellas to the law, there's going to be lots of questions and paperwork and a terrible black eye for Billy Vail and my whole damn department," he wearily muttered to himself.

Reaching a decision, Longarm used his good right arm to drag Berry's body out of its grave, across the ranch yard and the porch, and into the shot-up cabin. Next came the body of Jim Denton, followed by all the deceased members of the Quick gang.

When Longarm finally had them laid out inside, he was exhausted. He reached for a cheroot and a match. Longarm struck his match with a thumbnail and lit the cheroot. He puffed on it for a minute, and then nodded his head as if to confirm his decision.

"*Adios*," he said, walking over to a kerosene lamp and batting it to shatter and spill across the now-crowded floor. Then, as he passed on out the door, he tossed the cheroot back into the cabin.

Longarm was halfway across the yard when he heard the soft *whoosh* of flame sucking up the fuel. He turned all the horses loose except for the team that was already hitched and his own fine sorrel. He loaded all the rifles and saddles and whatever other gear he could find of value and struggled up into the wagon.

"Next stop, Wayout," he said quietly as he drove away from the funeral pyre and the flames that licked greedily toward the blue Nevada sky.

# Chapter 18

It was a long, hard trip back to Wayout, and Longarm debated the wisdom of riding in a wagon rather than a saddle during every bumpy mile. But the rifles and gear that had belonged to the Quick gang were worth a lot of money, and Longarm wanted it all to go to the daughter of Heck Wilcox. So far, Longarm believed Heck guiltless of any crimes. Admittedly, he had been involved with capturing One-Eared George and his gang, but he hadn't participated in their beating and murder. Other than that, Heck was still blameless, although it sounded as if he might be desperate enough to circumvent the law in order to raise money for his daughter.

When Longarm arrived back in Wayout, he caused a big stir. People came boiling out of the tents and gathered around the wagon as Longarm drove it up to the old feed supplier, who was still smoking his yellow corncob pipe.

"I've three hungry and thirsty horses, old-timer. How much will it cost me to take care of them?"

"You got a pile of saddles, rifles, and pistols in

that wagon. What happened to the outlaws that owned 'em?"

Longarm shook his head. "Ugly story."

"You're the only one left, huh. And you ain't looking too damn good with that shoulder."

"I'll be all right. Are Wade Quick and his brother in town?" The man looked up the street and puffed on his pipe for a few moments. Then he removed the pipe, pointed its stem past Longarm, and said very directly, "I don't know."

Longarm twisted around, understanding that the old man had pointed at one of the tents. In that way, he'd told Longarm that the Quick brothers were in town and where. "Thanks. Take your pick of a rifle. Any one except mine, which is in that saddle boot and had best be there when I return."

"What about that double-barreled shotgun?"

"I may need that," Longarm said. "Take a rifle or a pistol, holster, and cartridge belt. Any you choose."

"Obliged," the old man said, hopping down from his hay wagon with surprising agility and then hopping back up into the wagon that Longarm was driving. He lifted a well-oiled Colt from its holster and turned it this way and that for a close inspection. "I like this rig."

He'd chosen Jim Denton's gun, holster, and cartridge belt. "Good choice," Longarm said, easing down off the wagon. He hefted and gasped from the stab of pain in his wounded shoulder. Setting the shotgun back into the wagon bed, he drew the old man aside from the curious crowd and spoke to him in a low voice.

"Are the Quick brothers wounded?"

The man nodded.

"Dying?"

"Wade is going to pull through."

"Second tent on the right?"

"Yep. Can I share the reward?"

"No," Longarm said, "but you can take that fine shotgun in addition to the pistol. You'll either be the best-armed man in Wayout, or you can sell 'em for a pretty good price."

"If you used the shotgun to kill Wade and his brother, it'd bring me a lot more money."

Longarm shook his head. "Sorry. I'm going to have to do this with my six-gun."

"Fair enough, Marshal Long. There's an old boy campin' out in the brush that is a pretty good doc. You want me to bring him in to take a look at that shoulder?"

"If I make it, sure."

"Okay, I'll send someone for him. Good luck!"

"Thanks," Longarm said, " 'cause I'm sure going to need it."

Longarm walked up the street and the crowd fell in behind him. He wished that they would go away, and guessed that he should have told them to disperse. But he was tired and weak from loss of blood and trying to concentrate on the two outlaw brothers that he knew were hiding in that tent.

Longarm fooled the whole town when he stopped outside the tent next to it, then ducked inside the makeshift saloon.

"Wrong tent," the bartender said nervously. "The Quick brothers are laid up next door."

"Yeah, I know." Longarm went over to the spittoon where Jim Denton had dropped his federal officer's badge. He bent over and peered inside, then looked up at the bartender. "What did you do with it?"

"Here you go," the bartender said, reaching under the back bar and then setting Longarm's badge on a bar rag. "As you can see, it's all polished up. Marshal Long, I'm only asking ten dollars for it."

"It's worth a whole lot more," Longarm said, "but it's never been for sale."

Longarm pinned the badge to his lapel, then went outside. The crowd was still waiting for the anticipated shootout between himself and the Quick brothers to begin.

Longarm raised his right index finger to his lips. The crowd, which had already been hushed, grew very quiet. Longarm drew his gun and walked over to the tent. Taking a deep breath, he whipped its canvas fold aside to discover both the Quick brothers asleep on army cots.

Longarm stepped inside and took their gunbelts. He looked at the younger man and saw that he was dying of a gunshot wound in his gut. The kid didn't look to be twenty years old, and he must have been suffering terribly until he'd lost consciousness. Wade was badly glass-cut around the head and face, but otherwise appeared unhurt except for a splint on his lower right arm indicating that he'd broken his wrist or forearm when he'd jumped through the cabin window.

"Wake up," Longarm ordered.

Wade started into wakefulness and Longarm dragged the man to his feet. "You're under arrest for murder, stagecoach robbery, rape, and a whole lot more crimes."

"Well . . . well, who the hell are you?" the outlaw gang leader blurted out.

Longarm pointed to his shiny badge. "Deputy United States Marshal Custis Long. You're under arrest. Fall to your knees and put your hands behind your back."

"You taking me in?"

"Do as you're told."

"What about my brother?"

"If you got any prayers, say 'em for the kid because he's a goner."

Wade Quick twisted around to look at his brother. When he looked back up at Longarm, there was desperation in his eyes. "I can't just leave him to die alone!"

"Then I'll have his cot hauled out into the street so the townspeople can watch him die. It'll remind the slackers and troublemakers what happens to outlaws."

"But . . ."

"On your knees, dammit! I'm out of patience!"

Wade Quick dropped to his knees, and now Longarm realized that he didn't have anything to handcuff the man with. "Back on your feet!"

"What the hell?"

Longarm shoved his captive outside. "Anyone got a rope to tie this fella up with for the time being?"

A half-dozen people offered to get ropes.

"Looks like you and your gang weren't too popular in these parts," Longarm said with a tight smile.

"They liked us as long as we were buyin' the drinks," Wade said bitterly. "Where are you taking me?"

"I'm not sure," Longarm said. "But you can thank your lucky stars that it's me that caught you and not Denton or Berry."

"Who are they?"

"Never mind," Longarm said as a kid rushed up with a rope. "There will be plenty of time for explanations later."

He tied Wade Quick securely, and then marched him down the street of Wayout until he returned to his wagon. "Old-timer, I'm going to tie this jasper to the wheel. I've already given you enough firepower to watch over him while I wait for that doc friend of yours, get some food on my belly, and take a nap."

"Can I have another six-gun?"

"Sure," Longarm said. "But that's the last."

The old man cackled with delight. "Boy, oh, boy! This is sure my lucky day!"

Longarm walked away, not willing to field the questions that were coming at him from the big and excited crowd. He wasn't exactly sure what he would do next or even where he would go, except that before anything else, he wanted to find Heck Wilcox before that crazy old man really did run afoul of the law.

"Marshal?" a youth called, rushing into his path. "I'd like to come along and be your deputy."

"I can't let you do that," Longarm said. "It'd be on my conscience if you got hurt."

"But I'm a man! I can take care of myself!"

Longarm stopped and looked closely at the boy. "How old are you?"

"Sixteen."

"Take a look in that tent where the Quick brothers were sleeping. There's a kid in there dying of a bullet to the gut and I don't think he's much older than you are."

"I'm no outlaw," the youth said sullenly.

"And you're no lawman," Longarm said in a gentle voice before he passed on by.

# Chapter 19

Longarm was in passable shape the following morning. Wayout's sagebrush sawbones had proven to be a little more capable than most frontier doctors despite his poor circumstances. He'd cleaned and bandaged Longarm's bullet wound and then had given him some extra medicine.

"Instead of riding out after Garn Tilford," the doctor-turned-prospector had groused, "you ought to be resting that shoulder or it'll break open again and you'll lose even more blood. In fact, you could damn well bleed to death."

"I'll be careful," Longarm promised. "But why are you wasting your time prospecting when you could make a decent living in medicine?"

The doctor was a robust man in his forties, with a deeply tanned face and a miner's heavily calloused hands. "A doctor has to live with too much death. I just practice when there is an emergency or I need a few dollars as a grubstake."

He winked. "Don't let it get around, but I'm counting on striking it rich someday, Marshal."

"You and every other prospector I've ever known."

The doctor shrugged with an air of tolerance. "I understand your skepticism and freely admit that I've contracted gold fever, for which there is no medical cure. And maybe I will die penniless out here with a rock pick in my hand. But that's my choice."

"Sure it is," Longarm said, "but it's still a waste of education and talent."

The doctor didn't have an answer for that, and Longarm didn't press the issue. Obviously, this man had once received excellent medical training, but had fallen victim to gold fever like so many others. It was a shame, but hardly unusual.

Longarm wasn't the only one who was in pain this morning. Wade Quick was miserable with his broken forearm and his glass-cut face. The outlaw's eyes radiated hatred when Longarm said they were leaving Wayout before his kid brother could finally expire of acute lead poisoning.

"He could hang on for a couple more days," Longarm explained, "but there's no point in watching him suffer."

"Well, then who's gonna make sure that he gets a proper burial?"

"I'll pay for it," Longarm offered as Quick climbed up into the wagon.

Longarm rifled through his coat and pants, and realized that he was finally running short of money.

"Hang on," Longarm said. "I'd almost forgotten your horses. Where'd you leave them?"

"Up the street at the livery."

"Are they any good?"

"Hell, yes! Me and my brother wouldn't ride plugs."

"That's what I was hoping you'd say," Longarm told the insulted outlaw.

He left Wade under guard and went down the street to claim the two horses that the brothers had used to escape.

"Here they are," the liveryman said. "The Quick brothers always rode damned good horses."

"I can see that. And horses are something I've got plenty of right at the minute. You want to buy them?"

"How much?"

"Thirty dollars each. And that's cheap."

"I'll give you fifty dollars for the pair."

"Sold," Longarm said. "What about their saddles?"

"I might go ten dollars each. They're not worth much. Them brothers never did take good care of their gear."

Longarm went over to look at the saddles. "You're right, they're beat to hell."

"Anyone ever find all the money those boys took off the stagecoaches?" the liveryman asked.

"Nope. I expect they've hidden it somewhere around their ranch, but I didn't have time to search."

"Might be easy to find."

"I don't think so," Longarm said. "Their cabin burnt to the ground. Either the money they stole went up in flames or they've buried it outside."

Longarm took the liveryman's seventy dollars and went back to claim his prisoner. Before he got there, the old horse-feed man came rushing up all excited and waving a pair of saddlebags. "I got some mighty big news, Marshal!"

"Did my prisoner escape?"

"Naw, there's a small army guarding Wade. But look!"

The old man opened the saddlebags and showed Longarm that they were stuffed with greenbacks. "There's seven hundred thirty-seven dollars in these bags, Marshal!"

"They belonged to Jim Denton," Longarm said, taking the saddlebags.

"Denton is dead. Can we split his money between us?"

Longarm peeled off a hundred dollars for the man. "You could have kept all this cash for yourself and I wouldn't have known the difference."

"You wouldn't have?" The old man's face dropped. "Jezus! And I thought you knew and was just getting careless."

Longarm could see how disappointed he was, and so he gave him an extra fifty dollars. "Cheer up," he said, patting the man's thin shoulder. "You've been well rewarded since I've come to this town."

"Yeah, I have for a fact," he admitted. "I'm going to sell out here and move to California and grow oranges."

"You are?"

"Yep. My teeth are real bad and I can't hardly chew anything solid anymore. I read somewhere that oranges are the world's most perfect fruit."

"I wouldn't know about that," Longarm said, "but you sure can grow them sweet in California. Good luck to you, old-timer."

"Good luck to you, Marshal."

Longarm rebuckled the saddlebags, wondering if the cash was the Eagle Peak money that Denton had gotten by killing One-Eared George and his friends. It was also possible that this was other reward money that Denton and Berry had collected since handing in their badges. Longarm knew that there was no way that he would ever find out exactly where or how Denton had gotten so much money, and perhaps that was a blessing.

"Thanks, boys!" Longarm called to the men who had voluntarily guarded Wade Quick during his brief absence. "Here's twenty dollars for drinks on the house!"

The men were mostly prospectors, and Longarm's twenty dollars was a welcome sight. With whoops of celebration, they stampeded for the nearest tent saloon, leaving only Wade, the old man, and Longarm.

"Again, thanks for your help, old-timer," Longarm said as he prepared to leave.

Wade Quick looked up and glared at the old man. "I'm gonna get loose and kill this marshal. After that, I'm comin' back here and I'll cut your shriveled old balls off and make you eat 'em raw!"

The old man paled. He said in a small voice to Longarm, "You just watch this one 'cause he's pure poison."

"I'll watch him," Longarm promised. "Don't worry, because the only place he's going is the gallows."

Longarm climbed up into the wagon bed. "All right, Wade," he ordered, "roll over on your belly."

"No, dammit!"

Longarm booted the outlaw in the ribs almost hard enough to break them.

"Owww!"

"Roll over and put your hands behind your back!"

Wade rolled over and Longarm hogtied the man. It wasn't easy given his bad shoulder, but he was satisfied that the Nevada outlaw wasn't going to get free anytime soon.

"You keep an eye on him every damn minute!" the old man shouted.

"I will!"

"He's sneaky!"

"I know."

"Good luck in Quartzite. Hope you find your friend still alive."

"Me too!" Longarm called back as he drove out of Wayout.

Behind him, Quick cursed as he rolled and bounced against the wagon box. "I'll never swing from any damned rope, Marshal!"

"We'll see about that," Longarm replied. "We'll just see about that."

# Chapter 20

Getting to Quartzite was not easy but Longarm was determined, and stopped only to let the wagon team and his string of good saddle horses graze whenever he found adequate grass and water. His shoulder throbbed painfully but the wound did not reopen, and if it hadn't been for Wade Quick's constant bitching and moaning, the trip would almost have been bearable.

"Marshal, I've decided to cut your gizzard out and make you eat it raw!"

"Fine," Longarm said. "That's better than cutting my balls off and feeding them to me like you swore you'd do to that old-timer."

"I'll make you eat *them* too!"

Longarm just turned his head around and grinned at the outlaw. "You fellas are all talk and damned little show when it gets down to brass tacks. Hell, when the shooting started, there was eight of you at that ranch and only the three of us. But we evened the odds in one hell of a hurry."

"Yeah? Well, I don't know how you got into the cabin before the dogs caught wind of you, but—"

"We shot the dogs. Had to. By the way, I burnt the cabin to the ground."

"You what!"

"I burned it to the ground," Longarm repeated. "I didn't really want to, but it just seemed like the right thing to do at the time. Cremated all our friends."

"And about two thousand dollars cash!"

Longarm clucked his tongue with sympathy. "So that's where all that money you robbed was hidden."

Wade Quick was a strong and a tough man, but he sobbed with frustration. "Now I'm gonna cut your eyes out and make you eat them too!"

"My, my," Longarm said, "you sure are gonna feed me well. But I'm afraid that I'm not about to let that happen. You see, I've had a lot of practice bringing murderers like you to justice. I don't mean to brag, but when I hogtie a man and haul him to jail, he pretty much can figure he's going to find himself before a judge and jury."

"I'll never stand trial!"

"Oh, yes, you will," Longarm pledged. "I can see why you wouldn't want to stand trial, but you will anyway. How come you and your brothers turned out so rotten?"

Wade Quick was silent for a long time before he snarled, "It was the Paiutes. They killed my family."

"And so you took that as an excuse to kill other folks? That doesn't make much sense."

"You couldn't understand."

"I understand that hatred can turn people bad, and

I suspect that is what happened in your case, Wade. You and your brothers figured that since you had pain, you'd just spread it around to everyone else."

"Shut up!"

"Well," Longarm said, "there is no excuse for murderin' and rapin'. The judge won't think so either. You'll hang, and that's a fact."

"I wish to God that we were both standing in the street with guns in our hands. I'd drop you faster than dog shit."

"Yeah," Longarm said, "I hear that you're real good with a six-gun. They say you can throw a coin up into the sky and drill it before it hits the ground."

"That's right. What can you do?"

"I can't do any trick shots," Longarm admitted. "But I can generally hit what I aim at even when it's shooting back."

"You wouldn't even clear leather against me," Wade hissed. "You might not even get your hand on the butt of your gun before I put a bullet through your heart."

"I dunno," Longarm said easily. "A lot of men have tried to shoot me, and most all of them are now pushing up weeds in some lonesome cemetery."

Wade Quick swore under his breath, and Longarm let the man stew in his own poisonous juices. That night, unable to drive any farther without rest, he found a spring and decided that he had to get some sleep.

"We're going to hold over until morning," Longarm said, pulling in the team and then setting the brake. "All the horses are about played out and so am I."

He lashed Wade Quick to a pinyon pine tree, and

the outlaw howled like a scalded dog. "This thing is crawling with wood ants!"

"Well," Longarm said, "a man has to find his company wherever he can. If you don't bother the ants, they probably won't bother you. I'd suggest you just simmer down and relax before you get them all riled up."

Wade went crazy, fighting and struggling against his bonds, but he was helpless, and when he began to sob either in helpless fury or from ant bites, Longarm took pity on the man and untied him.

"Sit down next to the wagon wheel and I'll tie you to the spokes."

The outlaw couldn't follow the order fast enough. When he was tied beyond hope of escape, Longarm found them a sack of beef jerky.

"Open your mouth," Longarm said.

Wade opened his mouth, and Longarm shoved a strip of jerky between the outlaw's yellowed teeth. Wade chewed, eyes blazing with hatred. Longarm didn't care. He chewed his own meat slowly and when he'd swallowed it, he found a bottle of whiskey and took several good gulps.

"Want some to wash that jerky down?" Longarm asked.

Wade nodded. Longarm gave the outlaw a couple of swallows, then took pity and gave him a cheroot. They smoked in silence until Longarm's eyelids grew heavy. He found his bedroll and went to sleep without worrying about his captive getting free.

In the morning, Longarm fed his prisoner another strip of jerky, and then he loaded the man back into the wagon and drove on until he finally reached Quartzite.

"Looks about like every other mining camp in this state," Longarm drawled.

"I got friends here! They'll take care of me!"

"Thanks for the warning," Longarm said. "I'm hoping to find a friend myself."

"Oh, yeah? Who?"

"His name is Deputy Marshal Heck Wilcox, and he's killed more men in gunfights than you and me combined."

"The hell you say!"

"I do say," Longarm replied. "And when he sees what a snake you are, I'll have my hands full just trying to keep you alive."

That quieted Wade Quick. The outlaw sat up and glared at the townspeople as Longarm drove down the dusty street looking in vain for his old friend and mentor.

Quartzite wasn't very big and when Longarm reached its end, he hauled the team to a stop and climbed down.

"Hey," he called to a passerby.

The man was dressed in a black suit, with starched white shirt, and collar, and sported a fancy red tie. He looked like a prosperous merchant or businessman. When Longarm called out, he stopped and turned around. "Sir, are you addressing me?"

"Yes. I'm a deputy United States marshal and my name is Custis Long."

"Marshal, what can I do for you?"

"I'm hunting for another deputy marshal named Heck Wilcox. He's on the trail of an outlaw named Garn Tilford."

"I'm afraid Marshal Wilcox found Tilford."

Longarm's smile faded. "He did?"

"Yep. Or more exactly, Tilford found him."

"What does that mean?"

The businessman shifted, suddenly unnerved by Longarm's glowering expression. "Well, Marshal, I . . . I don't quite know how to tell you this."

Longarm's hands shot out and he grabbed the businessman by his coat. "Tell me what?"

"Tilford heard that Marshal Wilcox was looking for him. So he and another outlaw, Jud King, sneaked into town and shot the marshal down in a clever ambush."

"Are you sure?"

The businessman struggled to free himself. "I'm terribly sorry! But your friend was hit at least five times from both sides of street. He was lured into a cross fire."

A sob escaped Longarm's throat and he felt as if the world had suddenly gone dark and cold. "Where is Heck?"

"We buried Marshal Wilcox about a week ago." The businessman swallowed noisily. "I'm . . . I'm real sorry, Marshal Long. If it eases your mind, I can honestly say that your friend died instantly. One of the bullets hit him in the side of the head. The town doctor said that Marshal Wilcox was dead before he hit the street."

Longarm released the businessman and closed his eyes, and a long, powerful shudder ran the length of his body. He sniffled, roughly scrubbed his knuckles across his eyes, and said, "Where is Heck buried?"

The businessman straightened his coat, then pointed. "A couple of hundred yards to the north of that hotel you'll find the Quartzite cemetery. Marshal Wilcox didn't have any money so the undertaker took his horse, gun, and rifle in trade. Gave him a real nice burial. Marble headstone and everything."

Longarm scarcely heard the man. He staggered off in the direction of the cemetery and when he found the grave, tears were streaming down his cheeks. He removed his hat and sank to his knees. "Aw, dammit, Heck! Dammit anyway!"

Longarm was not a man to lose control of his emotions, but this was an exception. He bowed his head and silently wept for his old friend, the man who'd been more like a father than his real father and who had taught him much of what he knew about being a lawman.

Longarm lost track of time. The tears flowed until there were none left to give, and still he remained beside the fresh grave as the sun moved across the sky and headed toward the western horizon.

"Marshal," a voice hissed from behind, "since you loved that old man so much, I'm going to give you a one-way ticket to join him in Hell."

Longarm went cold inside. He did not turn his head, but his hand flashed to the gun on his left hip. He rolled sideways and drew in the same instant as Wade's pistol bucked.

Longarm's own Colt began to thunder. Wade was fast but he was a fool. He stood broadside offering a full target for Longarm, who did not squander the opportunity. Again and again Longarm's slugs ripped into the outlaw's body, driving him back until he tripped over a grave marker and spilled lifelessly across a burial mound.

Longarm emptied his gun and kept pulling the trigger in a blind rage until he slowly came to his senses.

Struggling to his feet, Longarm walked over to the dead outlaw and stared down at Wade's riddled body. Somehow he'd gotten loose, but Longarm didn't care much about that now. "At least you did get off the first shot," he grated. "Not that it mattered."

Longarm turned his back on the dead outlaw and returned to Heck Wilcox's fresh grave. "I'm sorry," he whispered. "If I'd been able to get here a week earlier, maybe you'd still be alive. I don't know. But I swear I'll get Garn Tilford and Jud King."

Longarm struggled to regain his composure, and then he added, "And I'll find your daughter and make sure she's well taken care of, Heck. I swear that I will."

He laid his hand on the grave and pressed it down hard enough to leave an imprint, then climbed to his feet and went to find the undertaker.

Ten minutes later, Longarm was towering over the man and saying, "You've got my friend's gun and holster. I want them."

"But he had no money! I claim them as repayment for my professional services. That gun and holster was small compensation for the cost I bore for Marshal Wilcox's fine marble headstone and flowers."

"You can keep his horse, saddle, and rifle, but not his six-gun," Longarm decided. "Also, I want any other personal items that Heck had on his person."

The undertaker dipped his pointed chin. "Yes, sir! But the marshal really had very little in his pockets other than a cheap brass pocket watch and chain, which I will give you because it's only value is sentimental."

"Did he have any letters or papers?"

"Yes, a letter. But I'm afraid that I've already disposed of it."

"Then undispose of it!"

"Yes, sir!"

The undertaker escaped into another room, and when Longarm followed, he saw the man madly rummaging around in a trash basket. Again rage filled Longarm, but before it could explode, the undertaker plucked a letter from the trash basket. "Here it is!"

Longarm took the letter. "I'm sure you read it."

"Why, no!"

"Of course you did," Longarm said. "Anyone would."

The undertaker's eyes dropped. "It was very upsetting, from a girl who says she is Marshal Wilcox's long-lost daughter."

Longarm nodded and read the letter.

*Dear Mr. Wilcox:*

*After all these years, my mother says that you are my real father and that you are a federal marshal. I know that it may come as a surprise that you have a daughter, and I'm sorry that I am not very strong or healthy, but my mother has already explained all that to you by now. I'm living with a Mrs. Peters in Reno and in need of some money for medicine. I know it is wrong to ask you for money but there is no one else who might help me. I am fifteen years old and have lived here for the last eight years. Mother tries but cannot help me. Please come when you can and do not expect too much when you see me.*

*Sincerely,*
*Miranda Wilcox*

A groan escaped Longarm's throat. He took a deep breath and struggled to maintain his composure.

"Marshal, can I get you something?" the undertaker asked solicitously. "A glass of whiskey perhaps?"

"Thanks."

The man darted off, and Longarm used a few moments of privacy to wipe his eyes dry and then square his shoulders. When the undertaker arrived with the glass of whiskey, Longarm downed it in a series of long, shuddering gulps.

"Are Tilford and King still in town?"

"They are staying at the Bonanza Hotel."

"And no one tried to arrest them for ambushing a federal marshal?"

"No, sir. Without question they would kill anyone who was foolish enough to interfere."

"Thanks," Longarm said, pulling his six-gun out of his holster and carefully reloading the weapon.

"Marshal, are you going to try and—"

"No," Longarm said, "I'm not just going to try and do anything. I'm going to kill Tilford and his friend, and you can have whatever money you find on their persons."

"Why, thank you!"

"Also," Longarm called over his shoulder, "there's a fresh body lying in your cemetery. It belongs to a no-good outlaw named Wade Quick. Bury him cheap."

The undertaker dashed after Longarm into the street. "But what if Tilford and King kill you?"

"Forward Miranda Wilcox's letter and all my cash to Miss Katherine Chambers care of the *Carson Courier* in Carson City. She'll know how best to help Miranda. As for yourself, keep my gun, horse, and saddle and then bury me cheap!"

The undertaker briskly rubbed his hands together with anticipation. No matter what the outcome between the marshal and the outlaws, he was going to collect.

# Chapter 21

Longarm had reinjured his shoulder during his gun battle with Wade Quick. He could feel it throbbing and knew that it had begun to bleed again, though not seriously. Still, the pain was distracting, and Longarm suspected that he would be feeling weak and perhaps even dizzy once his adrenaline stopped pumping. The time to face Garn Tilford and Jud King was now rather than later. Longarm hoped that they had not been alerted to his arrival, but that was probably too much to expect given the amount of attention he'd already received thanks to his cemetery shootout with Wade Quick.

As Longarm exited the undertaker's parlor, a big crowd surged around him, everyone asking questions about the gunfight he'd survived at the cemetery. Longarm ignored their questions and marched down the street. But at the entrance of the Bonanza Hotel, Longarm lost his patience with the curious and insistent crowd.

"I'm going to arrest Garn Tilford and Jud King for the murder of my friend Marshal Heck Wilcox.

That's it. There's nothing more to say."

Longarm started to turn around and enter the hotel, but a newspaper reporter with a pad and pencil touched his arm. "Please, Marshal Long. Can't you just give us a few more details?"

"There's nothing more to say."

"Well, what about that man you gunned down in our cemetery? Who was he?"

"His name was Wade Quick. Maybe you've heard of his gang of stagecoach robbers."

"Sure we have, but . . . "

"They're all dead now," Longarm said. "And if you don't stay out of my way, you might end up the same."

The reporter and the others recoiled, not sure whether or not to believe Longarm as he strode across the hotel lobby to the registration desk. The clerk had been reading an old San Francisco newspaper, but when he saw Longarm and the huge crowd pushing into the hotel, he quickly hid the paper.

"Yes, sir!"

"Marshal Custis Long. What rooms are Garn Tilford and Jud King using?"

"Tilford is in Room 201 and King is right across the hall in Room 202. But why . . . "

Longarm didn't wait to explain. These men had ambushed Heck and it was time for them to pay their dues. "Better call a doctor," he yelled back at the desk clerk before he took the staircase two steps at a time.

At the top of the stairs, Longarm drew his Colt and started down the narrow hallway. The damn floor creaked like crazy under his weight and Longarm swore silently. Room 201 was on his right, and

Longarm stopped to listen for any activity. Hearing nothing, he stepped to one side of the door and reached for the knob, which he began to turn.

Bullets ripped through the door just above the knob, exactly where an inexperienced or careless lawman would have been standing. Longarm's wrist was nicked by one of the bullets, but he scarcely noticed as he twisted the knob violently and threw the door open. Still not willing to expose himself to Tilford's fire by stepping into the doorway, Longarm showed only his arm and a thin slice of his face. He caught a glimpse of Tilford standing in his underclothes holding a smoking gun. Longarm dropped to one knee, stuck his Colt around the door frame, and drilled Garn Tilford in the gut.

From behind Longarm, Jud King threw his door open and yelled, "I'll kill you, you sonofabitch!"

He would have succeeded except that Longarm lunged into Tilford's room a moment before the outlaw behind him opened fire. Longarm rolled against the wall, expecting King to charge across the hall. Instead King ducked back into his room to slam and lock his door.

Garn Tilford was a hard-looking man in his thirties, with a full beard and black eyes that were already starting to glaze as he knelt on the floor of his room and tried to hold his gut with his left hand and raise his gun with his right.

"Why?" he choked.

"You killed Marshal Wilcox. He was like my father."

"He wouldn't leave me alone!" Tilford coughed and his eyes fixed on his shaking gun. It was taking all of his dying strength to raise the Colt.

"Put it down," Longarm ordered. "I've already sent for a doctor."

"Doctor be damned!" Tilford spat, raising the gun an inch at a time. "Ain't no doctor can save me. I'm a dead man."

Longarm could and probably should have shot Tilford to end his misery, but instead he retreated into the hall and closed the door. A moment later, he heard Tilford's gun explode in the room, and then he heard the sound of the outlaw's body as it pitched forward across the wooden floor.

"One down and one to go," Longarm said, face grim and set with determination.

Longarm tried the knob on Room 202 just to make sure it was locked. "King, I know you're in there! Come on out with your hands up and you'll go to trial. Fight me and I'll send you to hell!"

There was no answer, so Longarm stepped aside and shot the doorknob to pieces. He kicked the door open, realizing that he only had two bullets left in his six-gun.

Jud King was gone. The window curtains were flapping in the breeze and a woman was in King's bed with a sheet pulled up to her chin. She screamed when she saw Longarm, and he ducked back into the hallway and sprinted down the stairs. The crowd was still blocking the doorway, but when they saw Longarm flying across the lobby, they parted like the Red Sea.

Longarm jumped into the street just in time to see Jud King riding at him. The outlaw must have gotten confused in his panic to escape. King opened fire as he recognized Longarm, who calmly stood in the middle of the street. The outlaw's bullets were wild and Longarm raised his weapon, took careful aim, and shot Jud King through the forehead. The man batted at his face and then pitched off his racing horse. His left boot caught in the stirrup. The last that Longarm saw of King was his body bouncing wildly down the street before disappearing around a corner.

For a moment, time seemed to stand stone still in Quartzite. Suddenly, everyone flooded into the street to surround Longarm and, despite his protests, raise him up in the air and carry him off to the nearest saloon. It seemed to Longarm that they were a little carried away by their celebrating, but that only proved to him that Garn Tilford and Jud King had been damned unpopular.

# Chapter 22

Mrs. Peters lived on a pleasant, tree-lined avenue one block east of Virginia Street. On the day that Longarm drove a wagon into Reno, the sun was shining, the birds were singing, and everything seemed right with the world. Longarm's shoulder was still heavily bandaged, but it wasn't giving him much pain despite his recent hard Nevada travels. As he pulled up to the Peters house, he was filled with anticipation but also anxiety about his meeting with Miranda. Again he checked the address he'd been given, and then he set the brake.

Longarm saw an old woman with silver hair and a yellow shawl sitting beside a young girl on the front porch, and he knew at a glance that he'd found Heck Wilcox's daughter. Like her father, Miranda had a wide mouth, brown eyes, and a thick mane of unruly hair. She was pale-complected, and it was easy to see that she was tall but thin. When she saw Longarm, she stopped talking in mid-sentence, and Mrs. Peters turned to stare at the big man with his arm cradled in a sling and a shiny lawman's badge pinned to his leather coat slowly approaching her house.

"Afternoon, ladies," Longarm said in greeting as he removed his battered hat.

Miranda jumped to her feet, eyes wide with shock but also expectancy. "Are you . . . "

"No," Longarm said, "I'm sorry but I am not your father. He was my best friend and I'm sorry to say that he's dead, Miranda."

The girl blinked, and then she quickly turned away. Longarm took a deep breath and mounted the porch. "You must be Mrs. Peters."

"I am," the old lady said. "And who are you?"

"Deputy United States Marshal Custis Long, Denver office."

"Did you come all the way from Denver just to tell Miranda that her father is dead?"

"That, and to say that he was trying to make some money for her when he was cut down in an ambush. I settled the score and I've brought the money Heck wanted Miranda to have for medicine and her welfare."

Longarm reached out and touched the girl's shoulder. He felt Miranda shiver as he turned her around and studied her sad but pretty face. "Miss Wilcox, I have a letter that you sent to your father. I also have his pocket watch and a few of his personal things that I'm sure you'll want to keep."

"I don't even know what he looked like!" Miranda cried with anguish.

"Your father was a big, handsome man," Longarm said, "and a very good one. Heck Wilcox was one of the finest marshals that ever pinned on a badge."

She sniffled and forced a smile. "He was?"

"Yep. And he loved you, Miranda. He loved you so

much he almost gave up his profession in order to give you a great deal of money."

"How much?" the old lady asked with surprising directness.

"Enough," Longarm said, "to fix whatever ails Miranda and then to send her off to the best college in the country. That was what Heck wanted for her, Mrs. Peters."

"What a blessing!" the woman exclaimed, clasping her hands together. "I've a heart condition and I have to go to Sacramento and live. I'm a widow and I just couldn't . . . "

"I understand." Longarm placed his forefinger under Miranda's chin. "I've a lady friend in Carson City that you'd really like, Miranda. She and her father own a newspaper."

"They do?"

"Yep. Your father would have liked you to visit this woman and become her friend."

Miranda had thick eyebrows and they raised in question. "But why?"

"Because Miss Katherine Chambers is a lady and she's . . . she's very nice."

"Then I'd like to meet her."

"How about we do it now?" Longarm suggested. "It's a nice day and we can be there long before dark."

Miranda turned to Mrs. Peters, eyes pleading for permission. "Can I?"

Mrs. Peters studied Longarm's face and his heavily bandaged shoulder. "You look like a man that has been through a war, Mr. Long."

"I have, for Heck and Miranda."

"Then she may accompany you to Carson City."

Longarm heaved in gratitude. He remembered little of the idle conversation between him and Mrs. Peters that followed while Miranda hurriedly packed her bags. Miranda was frail, but she was excited, and they were on their way in no time at all.

"May I ask what ails you?" Longarm asked as they swung onto South Virginia Street.

"I have asthma and the medicine is expensive," she confessed. "My mother had it too when she was young."

"What happened to her?"

Miranda gazed off at the snow-capped Sierra Nevada Mountains. "She's tired, Mr. Long. Very tired. Ever since I was just a little girl, she's been tired and unable to keep me."

Longarm thought about that for several minutes. It sounded to him like a real sweet way for a daughter to speak about a mother who had conveniently abandoned her to other people's care and protection.

"Yeah, Miranda, we all get a little tired as we get older. In fact, I'm a little tired myself," Longarm admitted as they traveled on toward Carson City.

Watch for

**LONGARM AND THE GALLAGHER GANG**

188th novel in the bold LONGARM series
from Jove

*Coming in August!*